The Dance Dilemma

date him or dump him?

The Dance Dilemma

A Choose Your Boyfriend Book

CYLIN BUSBY

BLOOMSBURY
CHILDREN'S
BOOKS

Published by Bloomsbury U.S.A. Children's Books
175 Fifth Avenue, New York, NY 10010
Distributed to the trade by Holtzbrinck Publishers

Library of Congress Cataloging-in-Publication Data
Busby, Cylin.
The dance dilemma / by Cylin Busby. — 1st U.S. ed.
p.   cm.   — (Date him or dump him? A choose your boyfriend book ; 2)
Summary: As a teenage girl trying to find a date for the high school dance,
the reader makes choices to determine the outcome of the story.
ISBN-13: 978-1-59990-084-1 • ISBN-10: 1-59990-084-X
1. Plot-your-own stories. [1. Dating (Social customs)—Fiction. 2. High schools—
Fiction. 3. Schools—Fiction. 4. Plot-your-own stories.] I. Title.
PZ7.B9556Dan 2007   [Fic]—dc22   2006032261

First U.S. Edition 2007
Book designed and typeset by Amelia May Anderson
Printed in the U.S.A. by Quebecor World Fairfield
2 4 6 8 10 9 7 5 3 1

BLOOMSBURY
CHILDREN'S
BOOKS

For my boys,
Damon and August

The Dance Dilemma

$\mathcal{A}$nother morning, another outfit dilemma. You're trying to decide what to wear to school when you get a text message on your cell phone. It's from your best friend, Kelly.

What R U wearing 2day?

You have to laugh—it seems like she asks the same thing every morning.

Don't know yet.

You text back and continue to look in your closet. You don't want to end up wearing the same jeans as Kelly, which happens at least once a week, so instead you pick out a short skirt and a new top. Once you're ready to go, you text Kelly to let her know that she can wear her jeans today, if she wants. She texts you back:

Something REALLY big 2 talk 2 U about @ school

You're curious, but clearly she wants to tell you in person, so you grab your backpack and head out the door.

Once you get to school, you race to Kelly's locker for the news.

"So what's up?" you ask her, and then, looking at her outfit, you add, "Nice jeans."

She grins back at you. "You know how the big fall dance is coming up, right?"

Your mind starts racing. She doesn't have a date already, does she? "What, who asked you?" you exclaim.

Kelly rolls her eyes. "Please, I *wish* somebody had asked me! It's not that. The drama teacher, Mrs. Higgins, asked me if I would help decorate the gym this year."

You let out a sigh. That's not such big news. "So? You did that last year."

"Well," Kelly says, her eyes sparkling a little. "I'm not just helping this time. I'm actually heading up the whole dance committee. That means I get to pick the theme, put together a budget, everything. It's practically my dance!"

"Wow!" You're genuinely psyched for her. "That's amazing! You'll do great." Kelly is the most organized person you know, plus she has a flair for design, so you're sure the gym is going to look cool.

"You know what this means, right?" Kelly whispers, leaning in. "I have to go to the dance—whether I have a date or not." She looks at you just as the warning bell for first period rings. "And so do you!"

"Of course!" you agree. "But it would be nice to have a date, for a change," you add quietly, thinking about the cute guy in your study hall that you've had your eye on forever.

3

"Yeah...." Kelly looks off wistfully. "Hey, let's stop feeling sorry for ourselves. I've got a dance to plan!" she exclaims, and puts a smile back on her face. "And first period to get to."

You and Kelly head for the stairs but run into Mrs. Higgins on the way. "Good morning, girls," she says, pushing her funky glasses back onto her mop of curly hair. "Kelly, you're just the person I wanted to see. I've got three boys who want to volunteer for the dance committee—I told them they could help you set up the gym," she says. "I hope that's okay. I'll give you their names in class today."

As Mrs. Higgins walks away, you and Kelly lock eyes. "Boys?" you say together, then laugh. "I wonder who?" you ask.

"Please let there be at least one decent one!" Kelly adds, then grabs your arm. "I've got a brilliant idea! What if you join the dance committee, too? Think about it—three possibly hot guys, lots of after-school meetings and weekend setup. We might have dates by the dance!"

"Oh, Kel," you say, "I don't know." Kelly's always coming up with elaborate plans to meet boys—but you're not sure if these guys are even going to be your type. "I've got a lot of homework, a book report…I just don't know if I can."

Kelly's face drops. "Well, if you're too busy, okay. But it would be fun—" Just then the final bell rings. "Ack! Now I'm late!" Kelly yells. "Promise me you'll think about it? I want your answer after class," she calls to you as she races down the stairs.

You decide to join the committee. Go to 109.

You'd rather do something else after school. Go to 7.

The next day at school, Kelly meets you at your locker. "So, tell me all about this amazing dress you got for the dance!"

You smile. "It's light pink, fitted, strapless...," you start. "I don't know, you'll have to see me in it!"

"Mira says it makes you look like a Hollywood diva—she also told me about what happened with Kristen," Kelly says. "Uh-oh, look who's coming now...."

You close your locker and see Kristen and her friends, Dani and Amy, coming down the hall—the popular clique.

"Aren't you that girl from the store last night?" Kristen says, stopping next to you and Kelly. "The one who wanted to buy the same dress as me?"

"What a complete copycat," Dani says snidely.

"What a total loser," Amy chimes in.

"Come on, let's go," Kelly says, grabbing your arm.

"You better not wear that dress to the dance," Kristen calls after you. "Or you will be very, very sorry. Did you hear me?"

5

A few people in the hallway turn to look. You know that Kristen can make your life miserable if she wants to. And you're a tiny bit worried that maybe you shouldn't cross her. But the dress does look amazing on you, and you want to wear it. What are you going to do?

You decide to wear the dress anyway. Go to 134.

You'd rather return the dress and wear the other pink one instead. Go to 111.

"Sorry, Kel," you yell after her, "I don't think I need time to decide—it's just not my thing. We'll talk more later." Then you turn and dash toward your class. You're feeling bad about turning Kelly down, but the truth is you really are too busy to help out right now.

After class, you're still feeling bummed as you make your way over to your locker. "What's up?" says your friend Mira as she falls into step beside you. "School dance coming up—are you excited?"

You just shrug.

"Come on, where's your school spirit?" Mira says. "Let's go shopping after school and see if we can find some amazing dresses. That'll put you in a dance mood!"

"Okay," you agree. It does sound like fun—and Mira is always a blast to hang out with. "Where do you want to go?" you ask her.

"Maybe to the mall...," she says, suddenly blushing a bit.

"And maybe a certain incredibly gorgeous blond

football player will be grabbing pizza with his friends after practice?" you tease her.

"I'm not just going to see Owen!" Mira protests. "I really *do* need a new dress for the dance. Something nobody else will have."

"Well, if you're really looking for a cool dress, we should take the bus downtown and go to Polka Dots, that vintage store," you offer.

"The one where they play the awesome music?" Mira asks.

You nod. "And the one where Drew works." You both let out a little sigh.

"Drew," Mira repeats wistfully. "That dark hair, those eyes, and that smile. He's dreamy."

"Beyond dreamy. Perfection!" You giggle.

"So, is it Owen at the mall, or Drew at the vintage store? Where do we go?" Mira asks you.

You head to the mall. Go to 62.

You'd rather check out the vintage store. Go to 64.

Trying to keep the peace between Tyler and Kelly, you pipe in: "Let's take a vote and see how everyone else feels about 'Under the Sea' as a theme."

"Okay, that sounds fair," Kelly says. "Everyone in favor of 'Under the Sea,' raise your hand."

The two girls sitting in front of you raise their hands, and you do, too—not because you think it's the best idea for a theme, but because Kelly's your best friend. You're not about to side with some guy over her, no matter how good-looking he is.

"I can't vote because it's my idea," Kelly says. "Which means we have a tie. Three in favor"—Kelly nods at the girls—"and three not in favor." She glares at the boys. "So what do we do now?"

"Why don't we at least hear Tyler's idea?" one of the girls in the front suggests.

"Okay," Tyler says, clearly thinking out loud. "I'm picturing NASCAR. You know, racing and cars—or, wait! I just thought of something genius! How about a video-game theme, like *Sudden Death*—you know that game?" The girls in the room are at a loss. "We could get all kinds of fake blood and fake guns and stuff," Tyler goes on. "What do you think? Awesome, right?" he asks—and looks right at you!

You're over Tyler and ready to admit that his idea is horrible.
    Go to 13.
You still think he's cute and want to give him another chance.
    Go to 15.

You have to admit that the "Under the Sea" theme is pretty lame. Plus, you really want Tyler to like you! So you say, "Kelly, they *did* do that theme two years ago. Maybe we should come up with something new."

Everyone else on the committee agrees, but you can tell Kelly's feelings are hurt since she won't even look at you. "Fine. I suppose you have a better idea?" she snips.

"Uh, w-well...," you stutter. Now that she's put you on the spot, you can't think of anything to say.

Another girl in the group finally speaks up. "How about we stay with the water theme, just update it a little... something cool, like 'Atlantis'— you know, the lost underwater city?"

"Cool," Tyler chimes in, "we could build a whole underwater town in the gym—like underwater cars and Aquaman stuff." He grins at the girl, and she blushes back.

"Actually, I like it," Kelly says. "I don't know about underwater cars, but there's something here we can work with. Are we all in favor of an Atlantis theme?" she asks the group, and this time everyone agrees. "Okay, let's brainstorm some more ideas—underwater city sounds cool; what else?"

The guy on the football team raises his hand. Just as he starts talking, Tyler leans over and whispers in your ear, "Hey, do you know her?" He points at the girl who suggested the Atlantis theme.

"Yeah," you say. "That's Anna. She's in my grade. I have math with her," you tell him.

Tyler nods, and you can't help but notice again how adorable he is—his eyes are amazing this close up. He'd be a great date for the dance—and you can just picture how good you would look walking into the gym with him. Maybe you could get a green dress that would match his eyes....

"Do you know if she has a boyfriend?" Tyler suddenly asks, snapping you out of your daydream.

You happen to know that Anna's single, but what do you say to him?

You lie and say, "Yes, she's dating someone." Go to 17.
You tell the truth and admit that she's available. Go to 18.

"Well, what do you think?" Tyler asks you. He looks so proud of himself that it almost kills you to have to tell the truth.

"Actually, I think that might be the worst idea I've ever heard," you admit. You hear Kelly stifle a laugh.

"I have to agree," another girl says. "I'd much rather do the 'Under the Sea' theme than do race cars or video games."

"Unless anyone else has a bright idea for the dance theme," Kelly says, shooting Tyler a sideways glance, "we'll just go with 'Under the Sea.' Everyone agree?"

All the committee members nod, except for Tyler, who looks sort of hurt.

"Okay, then. We need to break up into three smaller committees to deal with all the work we have to do to get ready for the dance," Kelly says. "We'll have one committee for the music, one for refreshments, and another committee for decorations."

As she's talking, you notice someone else has come into the room, so you turn around to look. You're so happy to see that it's your best guy friend, Eddie! You didn't know he was going to be joining, so it's a nice surprise. You motion for him to sit by you and start whispering to him, catching him up on what's already been decided.

14

Go to 20.

"Well, what do you think?" Tyler asks you. You just sit there stunned—it's probably the worst idea you've ever heard, but how can you tell him that?

"I, uh, I just don't know that much about video games. Or NASCAR stuff," you finally mumble.

"I've got some videos of amazing races—and massive car crashes—at my place," Tyler says quickly. "You should come over sometime and we can watch them. Then you'll see how cool it could be for a theme."

"That's the dumbest idea I've ever heard," Kelly cuts in. "Car racing? At a school dance? Sorry, but no. Does anyone else have an idea?" she says, looking around the room.

"Your 'Chicken of the Sea' theme is the dumbest thing I've ever heard," Tyler shoots back. "Who cares? School dances are for losers, anyway. I wouldn't even be here if Mrs. Higgins hadn't made me come for extra credit."

You see Kelly's face fall—she didn't know that the boys had joined the group only to get extra credit. She'd thought they might actually be interested in helping out with the dance!

"This whole thing is lame," Tyler says, turning to you. "Want to get out of here? We can roll to my place and check out those videos."

Sounds like he's sort of asking you on a date, and you would love to hang out with him—but it means leaving the meeting early, which Kelly would not be too happy about.

You decide to leave with Tyler. Go to 22.
You'd rather stay in the meeting. Go to 24.

$\bigcup$ou pause for a second before answering him. "I think she's seeing this guy, but I can't remember his name," you finally say, and you can see from Tyler's face that he's bummed.

"Really, are you sure?" he asks you. "She seems cool."

You feel a twinge of jealousy—what's Anna got that you don't have? You're pretty cool, too! But if he's into her, you can't lie to him. Can you?

"Well…," you start to say. You can either fix it and tell him the truth or let him believe she's got a boyfriend (then maybe he'll notice you instead!).

You decide to tell him the truth. Go to 73.
You'd rather stick with your lie. Go to 74.

"I don't think she's seeing anyone," you admit. "In fact, I'm almost sure she's single."

"Yeah." Tyler nods, obviously excited to hear that. "Do you think she'd go to the dance with me?" he whispers over to you.

"I guess you'll have to ask her," you tell him. You're bummed out that your crush is digging someone else, but what can you do? You turn your attention back to what Kelly is saying.

"So we need to break into three committees— one will work on the music, another on refreshments, the third committee will do the decorating," Kelly says, looking at the group.

Just as she starts taking names for the two groups, someone plops down in the chair next to you. It's your best guy friend, Eddie, and you're so happy to see him!

"Hey, I didn't know you were going to be here!" you say.

He shrugs. "Kelly sort of 'encouraged' me to help out."

"She has a way of doing that!" you laugh.

"So, I'm late—what did I miss?" Eddie asks, and you tell him about the theme choice, and how there will be three committees. You two start talking about which committee you want to be on....

19

Go to 20.

"I'm into the refreshment thing," Eddie says to you. "Wanna do that committee with me? We'll get to hang out…," he says, looking away shyly. You've noticed that he's been acting funny lately—Kelly is convinced that he has a secret crush on you, but you're not so sure.

"I'll do the decorating committee," the guy from the football team volunteers. You glance over at him and wonder why you've never noticed him around school—he's actually kind of hot, with short red hair, broad shoulders, and a killer smile.

"What's your name again?" Kelly asks him.

"I'm Sean," he says. "And I'm supposed to tell you that Mr. Marshall said he would help out with the decorating committee, too—he's the new art teacher."

"Right," Kelly murmurs, writing his name on her clipboard. "Great, I'm sure Mr. Marshall will have some amazing decorating ideas." She shoots you a knowing look—you two have already discussed Mr. Marshall at length! He just started teaching at the school and he's really young—and really cute—for a teacher. All the girls have crushes on him.

"Okay, I need more people for the decorating committee and a couple more for the refreshment committee—what do you guys want to do?" Kelly asks, looking at you and Eddie. It's either the decorating committee (with Sean and Mr. Marshall) or the refreshment committee with Eddie. Both sound really fun. Which should you join?

You pick the refreshment committee with your best guy friend. Go to 28.

You join the decorating committee with hottie Sean and Mr. Marshall. Go to 30.

You and Tyler get up quietly to leave as the group continues discussing theme options.

"Where are you guys going?" Kelly asks when you're halfway to the door.

"We're out of here!" Tyler says, opening the door and stepping into the hallway ahead of you.

"He has some NASCAR videos to show me," you say lamely, looking at Kelly's face for a reaction. She's obviously not happy.

"Good for him," she says. "Can't you guys watch videos later? We're trying to decide on a dance theme. The meeting isn't over yet." She puts one hand on her hip and stares at you.

"You coming?" Tyler says, holding the door for you.

"Sorry, Kelly" is all you can manage to say before you step out. You feel bad leaving the meeting, but since you went only to meet guys, maybe Kelly will understand—you did meet a guy, after all!

"Whew! What a waste of time," Tyler says, closing the door behind you. "But now I have to find another way to earn some extra credit. My parents won't be too excited if I get a D on my next report card."

"Wow, you're really doing that badly in school?" you ask him. Then you get a great idea—a way for you and Tyler to hang out more! "Maybe I could, I don't know…help you, tutor you or whatever?" you say.

"That's okay, my girlfriend is already helping me with my homework. But thanks," Tyler says. Before you have time to react, his cell phone rings. "Oh man, this is her now—I forgot, I'm supposed to meet for homework at her place," he says. "Sorry, we'll have to do those vids another time, okay? See ya later." He waves to you as he walks away, leaving you standing outside the meeting alone.

23

Kelly's way too angry at you for you to go back in there. And now it's clear you never even had a chance with Tyler—that's the last time you pick a guy over your friend! Could this day get any worse?

END

If you want to try the meeting again, go back to 15.

"I can't leave right now," you tell Tyler, laughing a little. "We're in the middle of a meeting. Maybe we can watch the videos another time?" Sure, he's hot, but you're getting the feeling he may be too wacky and spontaneous for you!

"Okay, I guess you're right," Tyler mumbles, shrugging it off. "Another time." He scoots down in his seat—looks like he's planning to stick around, too. Maybe to hang out with you!

"Let's get back on track here, people," you hear Kelly say. "We still need a theme for this dance."

"What about an updated version of the 'Under the Sea' theme?" a girl in the group asks. "Like 'Atlantis' or something?"

"I like that!" you say.

"Yeah, I guess it could work," Tyler says reluctantly, turning to you with a smile. Maybe he's over the NASCAR incident and will actually help you guys plan the dance. You'd love for him to be involved.

Just then, someone sits down beside you. It's your best guy friend, Eddie. "Hey!" He grins.

"What are you doing here?" you ask him.

"Kelly asked me to come and help out. She was worried there wouldn't be enough guys in the group," he explains, looking over at Tyler.

"Now that we have a theme," you hear Kelly say loudly, "we need to split up into committees to get things organized. We'll have one committee for music, one for refreshments, and another for decorating. Volunteers?" she asks the group.

Tyler turns to you, "Wanna be on a committee with me? We could do the music. I'm a musician, so that's perfect for me."

You look at him quickly. There is something really adorable about him, but you're not sure—his idea for the dance theme was bizarre, and he totally overreacted when other people didn't agree with him. But maybe you should give him a second chance?

25

He's too odd for you and you want to be on a different committee. Go to 20.

You decide to join the music committee with Tyler. Go to 31.

When Chris reaches for your hand, you know it's wrong—he's got a girlfriend! But he's so adorable, and you've been crushing on him forever.

He leans in and kisses you again, this time on the lips. "I think you're so pretty," he whispers to you.

"What about your girlfriend?" you say before you can stop yourself.

Chris leans back in his chair and lets out a sigh. "Things just aren't working out with Amy," he admits. "I'm about to break up with her, actually. All we ever do is fight. It's annoying." He looks so serious, you start feeling sad for him.

"I'm sorry." You don't know what else to say. "I hope it all gets worked out."

"Yeah, I don't really want to talk about it—not with you," he says, meeting your eyes. "Let's just forget about all that and have fun tonight." He reaches for your hand again and leans in to kiss you.

You can't help thinking about his girlfriend—even though they're about to break up, she probably wouldn't love the idea of you kissing her guy at the movies. But Chris did say that things weren't going well—so maybe she knows it's over between them. He's allowed to do what he wants, and so are you, right?

You want to start seeing Chris, even though he still has a girlfriend. Go to 84.

You decide he's a creep and you're not interested. Go to 75.

"I'll do the refreshment committee with you, Eddie," you turn to him and say.

"Cool," he says back. "We'll do refreshments," he says to Kelly, and you notice he's blushing.

"Can you two work out a time to meet? I'm putting you in charge of that group," Kelly says quickly, making a note on her clipboard.

"Sure," you say, turning to Eddie. "When do you want to get together?"

"Uh, whenever you want is good," he mumbles.

"Maybe tomorrow after school?" you suggest. "We can just meet here if you want."

"Or we could go to that cool coffee shop downtown, the new one. I've been wanting to go there with you, anyway," Eddie says. He gives you a funny look.

"That sounds good," you say.

"So it's a date," Eddie says quickly, smiling so that his dimples show. "I mean, not a *date* date, but a meeting date. You know what I mean," he backtracks.

Something is definitely up with him, and you want to know what it is. Do you feel like you can ask him? Or would you rather just wait and see what happens tomorrow?

You decide to ask him why he's acting so awkward. Go to 34.
You'd rather just ignore it. Go to 36.

"Put me down for decorating," you tell Kelly, and glance over at Sean.

"Great! You and Sean can decide how to work it out with that group and with Mr. Marshall," Kelly says, jotting down some notes on her clipboard.

"Eddie, I'll see you later," you say, moving over to sit by Sean.

"I have to go to football practice right now," Sean says, barely looking at you, "but I can meet you tomorrow after school."

"No problem, I'll see you then," you say quickly as he grabs his backpack and races out the door.

"Okay, well, 'bye," you say, watching him leave. You let out a little sigh. How could you think that you'd have a chance with a guy like that? Oh well, at least you'll get to hang out with him at the decorating meeting tomorrow.

Go to 174.

"I'll do the music committee," you tell Kelly.

"Me, too," Tyler says.

"Okay, you are the only two volunteers for that group, so try to work it out on your own. Let me know if you need any help," Kelly says, making notes on her clipboard.

"We can meet over at my house," Tyler offers. "Actually, we can still catch the bus and head over there now, if you have time."

"Let's go and get started," you say. "We have a lot of planning to do."

As you get on the bus, you two talk a bit more, and you start to think that perhaps Tyler isn't as crazy as you thought. Maybe he was just embarrassed when everyone hated his idea.

When you get to his house, you're surprised to see that his room is full of musical equipment—two guitars, a keyboard, an amplifier, even a drum set. The walls are lined with posters of bands and musicians.

"You're into music, huh?" you say jokingly.

"Just a little bit," he jokes back. "That's why I wanted to be on the music committee. Here, check this out," he says, picking up one of his guitars. He sits on his bed and begins playing a really beautiful, simple tune. When he starts singing, you find yourself lost in the words. He's amazing! Who knew he was so talented? You watch him playing the guitar and realize that he's in another world—he really is a gifted artist. When the song is over, he pauses, then looks at you for a reaction.

"I don't know what to say," you admit.

"That bad, huh?" Tyler smiles.

"No, that *good*—you're so incredibly talented. How did you learn to play like that? And what song is that? Did you write it?" Suddenly, you have so many questions.

Tyler blushes. "I've been into music since I was a kid, and yeah, I wrote that. I've written a lot of stuff. I'm in a band—sort of. We just started playing together, but I think we're pretty good...." Tyler trails off, obviously embarrassed talking about himself. "Anyway, let's talk about the music for the dance."

"Right," you say. "Do we want a DJ or should we hire a band?"

"There aren't any cool bands around here, so I think we'd have to do a DJ," Tyler says. "Unless...you think my band is good enough to play at the school dance!" he jokes, but there's a sparkle in his eye—you can tell he'd love the chance to play a big party with his band.

"I don't know if I'm a good enough judge of music to make that decision," you admit, watching Tyler as he starts strumming his guitar again.

"Maybe you should come and see us play?" he says, his dark green eyes meeting yours. You feel a shiver go down your back. There's definitely something between you two. But do you trust yourself—and your true instincts—enough to make a call on the music for the dance? What would Kelly say if you told her that you wanted Tyler's band to play the dance just because you're into him? And what would you do if they actually turned out to be awful? Maybe you're in over your head....

33

_____ ℓ _____

You decide to ask Kelly if Tyler's band can play at the dance.
Go to 42.

You'd rather just be on a different committee. Go to 173.

The next day after school, Eddie's brother, Matthew, gives you guys a ride to the coffee shop. You've come prepared for the meeting with a notebook and some ideas of what kinds of refreshments you want to have at the dance, but you're also thinking it's time to talk to Eddie about why he's been acting so uncomfortable around you.

"He's got a massive crush on you!" Kelly told you when you brought it up at lunch. "I noticed it this summer. Every time we went to the pool, he couldn't take his eyes off you. And have you seen how he can't even talk when you're around—"

"Maybe," your friend Mira interrupted, "but maybe not. What if it's the other way around—and he thinks you have a crush on him? You guys *have* been friends for a while. Have you given him any signs that you like him?"

You're still thinking about that as you sit down with Eddie and your mocha latte at the coffee shop. Things used to be so easy and fun for you guys, but now suddenly everything is awkward.

"So, let's talk about the dance," Eddie says. "I mean, not the dance, but the refreshments for the dance, you know...." He trails off and looks down into his mocha nervously.

You just can't take the tension anymore! You have to find out what's up. "Look, I don't even know how to ask you this, but is there something up with you—with us? I feel this strange vibe every time I'm around you lately, and I don't know why," you finally say.

"That's funny, because I feel the same vibe every time I'm around *you*," he admits, looking into your eyes. You feel funny in your stomach for a second, but then you remind yourself—this is just Eddie!

"What do you think is going on?" you ask him, meeting his gaze.

He grins and gives you a shrug. "I don't know. Maybe we're meant to be more than just friends," he suggests. He reaches across the table and lightly takes your hand in his. "What do you think?"

You tell Eddie, "I'm sorry, I don't think I can date a friend."

Go to 173.

You want to give a relationship with Eddie a chance.

Go to 44.

The next day, Eddie stops you in the hall at school. "My brother said he can give us a ride to the coffee shop after school today. You know, to talk about the dance—I mean to talk about the planning for the committee and everything," he rambles on nervously.

"Sounds good. Where should we meet?" you ask him.

"I guess outside. Or maybe you want to come over to my house first? Whatever you want to do. I don't know why I just said that!" he laughs, and meets your eyes for a second. "We should meet outside, right?" he asks you.

"Whatever is easiest for your brother is fine with me." You shrug. You're slightly annoyed at how strange Eddie has been acting lately. Making plans with him used to be really easy, and hanging out with him was fun. Now everything is so awkward.

"Okay, then I'll see you outside, after school," Eddie says quickly, and turns to go. He takes a few steps, then turns around. "Oops! My next class is actually this way," he admits, heading in the other direction.

You just stand there shaking your head. "What was that about?" Kelly says, coming up to you. "What's up with Eddie?"

"I wish I knew," you admit, and tell her how he's been acting lately.

"Uh-oh, sounds like somebody has a crush," Kelly says. "What are you going to do about it?"

"I don't know," you say. "What should I do? I like Eddie, but not *that* way."

"If you don't want to ruin your friendship, you'd better deal with it, and fast. Either you sit down with him and let him know how you feel or..." Kelly trails off.

37

"Or what?" You can tell by the look on Kelly's face that she's got a plan.

"Or set him up with someone else—that'll get his mind off of you!" she says, obviously so proud of her idea. Neither option is easy, but you've got to do something....

You decide to set Eddie up with one of your friends. Go to 46.

You're ready to tell Eddie you don't feel the same way
about him. Go to 49.

"*I* can help out with the fund-raising," you say, blushing. It's hard for you to meet Mr. Marshall's eyes, he's so cute!

"Great! So what's the theme for the dance?" he asks.

"We decided on an underwater theme," Sean answers him.

"I love it!" Mr. Marshall says. "Very retro. Now we need to come up with something just as cool for fund-raising. We can have a bake sale or something at the game on Saturday...." He trails off. "But that's so boring, isn't it?"

"Maybe something with water would be better, you know, to go with the dance. Water balloon dart throw or something?" Sean suggests.

"That's a good idea," you say, turning to him. He's not only adorable, he's also smart—a combination you cannot resist!

"I've got it!" Mr. Marshall says suddenly. "We'll do one of those dunking booths! Like at the county fair. You know, you get to throw a ball at a target, and if you hit it, the person goes splashing down into the water."

"Yeah, maybe we could get a couple of the teachers to volunteer to sit in the booth," Sean suggests. "I'd pay good money to dunk some of my teachers!"

"Perfect!" Mr. Marshall says. "An easy way to raise money. And maybe some students would volunteer to be dunked as well—just to keep things fair." He gives you a little wink, and you feel yourself blushing. "How about you?" he asks. "The drama department has this amazing old mermaid costume that you could wear, and people could pay to dunk the mermaid. Now that's an idea, right?"

You pause for a second. It all sounded pretty good until he suggested that. Would you dare put on a mermaid costume and go into the dunking booth? Maybe you should say you're too busy... but you do have a little crush on Mr. Marshall, and it seems like he wants you to do it.

39

───────────────○───────────────

You say that you're too busy to do the dunking booth.

Go to 40.

You'll give the dunking booth a try. Go to 51.

"$\mathcal{O}$n second thought, I only have enough time to help with the decorating. Sorry, Mr. Marshall," you tell him.

"That's okay, I should be able to find a couple of students who can help me with the fund-raising, and maybe you two can find a few more volunteers to help with the decorating?" Mr. Marshall asks. "I think it's too much work for just two people."

"I can ask some of the guys on the team," Sean says, "but we have a big game coming up this week-end, so I don't know how many of them can do it."

"I know a couple of people I can ask, too," you mention. "As long as we get four or five people who can do a few hours this weekend, I bet we can get a lot done."

"Sounds like a plan," Mr. Marshall says. "I'll meet you guys at the gym on Saturday morning and we'll get started."

"See ya," Sean says as you two walk out the door. "He's a cool teacher, huh?" he asks as soon as you're in the hallway.

"He seems great." *And he's so handsome*, you think—but don't say out loud!

"I wish I had more time to help out, but I've got a game on Saturday. I'm not even sure if I'll be able to make it over to the gym to decorate," Sean says.

"That's all right," you tell him, "I can make it, and I'll ask some friends to help."

"If you find enough friends to chip in, maybe you'll get done early and you can make it to the game, too," Sean suggests. "I'd love to see you there," he says quietly. You look into his face and notice, for the first time, that he has tiny adorable freckles across his nose. You can just picture him in his football uniform, those broad shoulders, out on the field....

41

"I'll have to see how things go," you say, but you already know what you want to do.

You decide to help decorate the gym on Saturday. Go to 54.

You blow off decorating to support Sean at his game.

Go to 58.

When you get home that night, you call Kelly to tell her how your meeting with Tyler went. "He's so talented," you tell her. "Have you ever heard him play the guitar? He's really good!"

"Sounds like you have a teeny crush!" Kelly laughs. "He seemed like such a weirdo in the meeting today. Are you sure he's cool?"

"He's an artist, you know. Aren't all real artists a little strange?" you ask her.

"I don't know," she laughs. "In between him playing his guitar for you, and you totally falling in love with him, did you guys manage to come up with any ideas for music at the dance?"

"Actually—and this might sound crazy, but just hear me out—I was thinking that Tyler's band could play at the dance. How cool would that be?" you ask Kelly.

"Are they any good?" she asks quickly.

"What do you mean? I just got done telling you that he's amazing on the guitar, so I'm sure they'll rock," you explain.

"Seems like a pretty big chance to take just because you have a crush on some guy," Kelly points out.

You still want to support Tyler's band's playing at the dance.

Go to 164.

You think Kelly is right, and you're in over your head.

Go to 168.

"*Maybe we like each other?*" you finally manage to say.

"I guess so," Eddie grins. "I just started feeling this way over the summer—it was really strange, like I would miss you when we couldn't hang out. Do you know what I mean?"

Something about the idea of dating Eddie makes you want to giggle. "Should we go on a date or something and see what happens?" you ask him.

"Let's go to a movie on Friday," Eddie suggests. "Maybe grab something to eat..."

"But that sounds like the same thing we always do!" you laugh.

"This time it would be different," he says, and he leans across the table. Before you know what's happening, his lips touch yours softly. And you feel your heart beat fast. But are you really into him, or do you just like the idea that he likes you?

"I want you to go to the dance with me—not as a friend, as my date," Eddie says, taking your hand across the table. You tell him...

"I don't know if I can date a friend." Go to 173.

"I'd love to be your date to the dance—let's try it!" Go to 141.

You're still thinking over Kelly's advice about Eddie as you're walking to your next class. "Hey, girl!" your friend Mira says, sliding up to you. "What's up?"

Suddenly, you have a solution to the problem! "Not much…," you tell Mira. "Hey, I was just wondering something. Would you like to be set up with one of my guy friends?"

Mira squints her eyes at you. "Well, maybe," she says, then giggles. "It all depends on who the guy is!"

"It's my friend Eddie. You know him a little, right?" you ask her.

She shrugs. "He's okay. Does he like me or something?"

"Well, there's only one way to find out!" you laugh as you both walk into your class and sit down. "Why don't you join the dance committee? Then you two can work together on the refreshment planning. I was supposed to do it with him, but you would be better at it," you say.

"Sure," Mira says. "Who knows, maybe I'll even get a date to the dance!"

"Great! Meet me and Eddie after school today, and we'll all go over to the coffee shop together."

Later that day, you meet Mira and Eddie on the front curb of the school. When Eddie sees Mira, he's surprised. "Hey," he says, "I know you from—"

"The pool this summer," Mira says, shaking his hand. "I'm Mira."

"Yeah," Eddie nods, looking at her face. Mira is so gorgeous, of course he's noticed her before! This might be easier than you thought.

"So you're going to join our committee?" Eddie asks, looking over at you. "We're supposed to help plan the refreshments for the dance."

Mira shifts her backpack nervously. "I definitely want to help. I just wish I knew if I was going to the dance—that would make it more fun, you know?" she says, shooting him a look.

"You mean you don't have a date?" Eddie asks, smiling. "I find that very hard to believe."

Mira looks down at her sneakers, blushing.

You can't believe your luck—they're totally hitting it off!

Just then, Eddie's brother drives up and honks

his horn. "Here's our ride!" Eddie says, opening the back door for Mira.

"Oh, you know what?" you say suddenly. "I totally forgot—I've got a chem lab meeting today." You hope Eddie will fall for the excuse.

"I thought chem lab was on Wednesday," Eddie says.

"Yeah, it usually is, but this is sort of a make-up lab thing—I'll explain later. You and Mira just go and have fun." You give Mira a wink that Eddie can't see, and she shoots back a big smile. "I'll see you guys tomorrow!"

You wave as Eddie's brother drives off with the two of them in the backseat, but they hardly notice, they're so into each other. Perfect—it actually worked! You feel like a huge weight has been lifted off your shoulders. Now you've taken care of the Eddie problem, but how can you still help out with the dance, too?

48

Go to 173.

$\mathcal{T}$hat afternoon when you meet up with Eddie, you know you have something really difficult to tell him. He's waiting for you outside the front of the school, and it breaks your heart the way his face totally lights up when he sees you.

"Hey, Eddie," you say sadly. "We need to talk."

"Okay," Eddie says, sitting down on the curb. He looks concerned. "Something wrong?"

You sit down beside him and decide that you'll just say it as fast as you can. "I've been getting this feeling from you lately, like maybe you have a crush on me or something...," you start.

"Actually, you're right—I do," Eddie says, trying to meet your eyes.

You quickly look down at your sneakers and take a deep breath. Now what? "Look, I really like you a lot," you start. "You know that already. And I think we're great friends. But I just don't feel that way about you," you admit. "I don't like you as a boyfriend. Do you know what I mean?"

You hear Eddie sigh next to you. "Then I guess

it's a mistake for us to try and work on the same committee together," he says. "Is that what you wanted to tell me?"

You just nod. You hate hurting him like this! "I can ask Kelly to move me to another group. But it's not so much the committee that I care about; I just hope we can still be friends. What do you think?" you ask him. You can tell by the look on his face that he's crushed.

"I guess we'll see what happens," Eddie says just as his brother drives up. He stands and grabs his backpack. "Later." As he gets into the car, he gives you a little wave that makes you want to cry. You sit and watch as they drive off, thinking about what you've just done. You feel horrible, but there was nothing else you could do, right?

50

Go to 173.

That weekend, when you meet Mr. Marshall at the school to help set up the fund-raiser, you're already regretting your decision to be part of the dunking booth.

"Here's that mermaid costume!" Mr. Marshall says, coming out of the drama club's costume closet. He's holding a small piece of shiny fabric that looks more like a scarf than an outfit. "This will be great! Go put this on while we finish filling up the dunking booth," he says.

You scoot into the girls' bathroom with the costume and look it over. It's tiny! And made out of some stretchy material that will be skintight on you. It takes you a minute or two to even figure out how to squeeze into it. The fabric is really beautiful—an iridescent blue-green that sparkles like the scales of a gorgeous sea creature. You shuffle over to the mirror in the bathroom to see how you look.

The top is strapless, coming up just to your

chest with a scalloped trim. The rest of the outfit hugs your every curve, down to the tops of your feet, where there's a cutout for you to walk (just barely!) with your feet hidden behind the big fake fin that attaches to the costume.

You manage to take tiny steps and work your way out of the bathroom and then, slowly, down the hall and over to the door that leads out to the school parking lot. Mr. Marshall is standing just outside, watching some kids fill the dunking tank over on the football field. "There you are. All ready?" he says when he sees you.

"Yeah," you laugh. "Sorry it took me so long. Like a real mermaid, I can barely walk in this thing." You motion down to your mermaid fin.

"Well, here," Mr. Marshall says, giving you his arm to lean on. "Let's get you out to the dunking booth to meet your tormentors, shall we?" You're a little bummed that he didn't say anything about how you look in the costume.

As you hobble along beside him, it's clear that it's going to take you forever to get across the parking lot, and you're kind of embarrassed

52

by all the stares from the other students. It would be a lot easier if Mr. Marshall just carried you, really. You glance up into his face. Do you dare flirt with the cutest teacher at school like that?

You want to ask him to pick you up and carry you. Go to 131.
You decide it's wrong to flirt with your teacher. Go to 170.

That Saturday, you arrive at the school gym, armed with all sorts of decorating supplies—streamers, balloons, and posters, all ready to hang up. A couple of other students meet you there, and everyone gets right to work. One guy brought some tunes and turns up the music for everyone to enjoy while they work.

As you climb up the ladder to hang another streamer, you realize that you're having a blast, but you're still bummed that you had to miss Sean's football game, especially when it seemed like he really wanted you to go. You start daydreaming about what you might have said to him after the game....

"That looks great!" you hear Kelly say from below, interrupting your silly fantasy. "You guys are all doing such an amazing job! I brought everyone some pizza, so why don't we take a lunch break?"

"Awesome!" one guy says, leaning the chairs he was setting up against one wall.

"It's out here in the hall," Kelly says. "And I

brought some sodas, too." One by one, everyone files out of the gym for lunch, leaving you on the ladder. You just want to get this last streamer hung up, and then you'll take a break, too. Once you get the end taped up, you head down the ladder, still bopping out to the music a little bit.

You dance over to the craft table to put down the tape and scissors but can't help yourself—the music sounds so good in the big empty gym, and you love this song…pretty soon you're dancing by yourself in the middle of the dance floor space, trying to copy some moves you saw in a hot music video. You close your eyes and spin—this song is amazing, it always makes you want to move! Then you hear something—someone clapping!

You stop dead in your tracks and see…Sean standing by the doorway of the gym! He crosses the floor to you, still clapping a little. "Nice moves," he says, smiling. He's wearing jeans and a white T-shirt and is carrying his football helmet—and he couldn't look cuter.

You're still a bit out of breath—and feel your face turning bright red. "I was just…" You stumble for an excuse.

"Just checking out the dance floor, making sure

it works and everything, right?" Sean jokes, and you can tell by the look in his brown eyes that he's teasing you.

"Yeah," you agree, grinning. You straighten your shirt and push your hair back from your face, trying to look at least halfway decent.

"Looks like the dance floor is okay, at least from what I saw," he says quietly, standing close to you. "You looked good."

"Yeah, right!" you laugh. "Hey, I thought you had a game today?"

"I do, in about an hour. I was just about to go suit up, but thought I'd come by here first to see how the decorating was going," Sean says.

56

"So, what do you think?" you ask him, glad to change the subject.

"I think this gym has never looked more beautiful than it does right now," he says, stepping in closer to you. "Because you're here." Before you can say anything, he leans in and kisses you softly on the lips, brushing your cheek with his hand.

"I should let you get back to work," he says, backing away from you. "I want the gym to look perfect...for our first date." He meets your eyes. "Okay?" he asks.

You don't know what to say. Is he asking you to the dance?!

"I'll come by after the game, if you're still here, so we can talk about the night of the dance—you know, what time I should pick you up, what color flower you like, all the important stuff," he says as he turns to go. Then he meets your eyes. "And save some of those dance moves for next Saturday night, okay?" He grins.

You watch him leave the gym, then jump up and down—you can't believe that your crush is now your date to the dance—yes! You can't wait to tell Kelly!

END

"What do you mean you can't come on Saturday?" Kelly says over the phone when you tell her. "You're on the decorating committee. I need you to come to the gym and help us out!"

"Sorry," you tell her. "Something else came up that I have to do."

"Like what? Something with your parents, something you can't get out of?" she asks.

"Actually, you remember that red-headed guy from our first meeting, Sean? He's on the football team?"

"Yes, I remember him." Kelly sighs. "And I don't think I'm going to like this...."

"He asked me to come to his game, so I'm going! Who knows? Maybe he'll even ask me to the dance!" You can't hide your excitement.

"You've got to be kidding me. You are blowing me off for some guy you just met?" Kelly sounds exasperated.

"Look, Kel, there are a bunch of other people on the committee—they can get it done. I just don't see why it's such a big deal." You wait for her to say something. "Kel?"

You look at your phone and see the words "call ended"—she hung up on you!

Not only is your best friend mad at you, but you're left to pick out the perfect outfit for the game all by yourself. On Friday night you spend an hour going through your closet. You want to look casual—after all, it is just a football game—but you also want to look amazing. Finally you pick out a pair of jeans that fit just right, a cool pair of low boots, and a fitted T-shirt that you can throw a jacket over if it gets chilly.

59

When you show up to the game on Saturday, you're missing Kelly more than ever. You wish she would come and sit with you in the stands, but she's too busy setting up for the dance—and besides, she's angry with you.

You find a place to sit and quickly scan the field for Sean—there he is! Number 12. He looks so good on the field, your eyes are glued to him until halftime. You make your way down the bleachers— might as well go and say "hi," right? After all, he did ask you to come. Maybe it will help him play better if he knows you're there!

"Hey, Sean," you say, sliding up behind the home team's bench. "You guys are playing really great today!"

"Hey, you came!" Sean looks surprised to see you. "I thought you had to decorate the gym today."

"I'd rather be here," you say, meeting his dark eyes for just a second.

"Awesome school spirit," he jokes. "I like it!"

Just then, a cheerleader with a high blond pony-tail bops over to Sean. "Here, sweetie, I brought you some water," she says in a baby voice. "You must be so, so tired." She pushes his sweaty hair back from his forehead and plants a kiss on him!

"This is my girlfriend, Dani," Sean says, looking embarrassed. "And this is…" He looks at you, obviously struggling. "Anyway, she's helping out with the dance committee," he says to Dani. You can't believe it—he didn't even remember your name!

"Awesome! I can't wait for the dance. Sean and I are totally going to be the king and queen this year, right, sweetie?" Dani says, plopping down on his lap and staring into his eyes.

You stand there for a second, watching them, then realize that they've completely forgotten you're even there. Great. Now your best friend hates you and the guy you have a crush on has a serious—and super lame—girlfriend. So much for that school dance!

END

If you want to help Kelly decorate the gym, go back to 40.

"This store always has the best stuff," Mira says, pulling you into an expensive dress shop on the second floor. The two of you caught the bus to the mall right after school, so you actually have some time to shop for dresses before the football team shows up at the food court.

"Look at this one." Mira pulls a short white dress off the rack. "You have to try it on!"

"I think it would fit better on you," you have to admit. "With your legs, you can always wear short dresses."

"Let's both try it," Mira says, grabbing two of the dresses and heading to the dressing room.

After you help Mira zip up her dress, you both stand in front of the mirror. The dress actually looks better on you after all.

"It's not right for me," Mira says, going back into her dressing room. "I don't want to shop anymore today. Now I feel fat," she whines. You're disappointed. You were really looking forward to finding a dress! Obviously, Mira just wanted to come to the mall to see Owen.

As the two of you leave the store, someone comes up behind you. "Hello, ladies," you hear a male voice say.

"Owen!" Mira squeals in mock surprise. "What are you doing here?" She tries to sound casual.

"Football practice was canceled today, so Chris and I are going to catch a movie," Owen explains.

Owen is great-looking, but in your opinion, his best friend, Chris, is even better—with his shaggy blond curls and brown eyes, he's got a surfer look that you can't resist.

"Hey, why don't you guys join us?" Chris says, looking right at you.

63

"Yeah, come to the movies," Owen begs. He's obviously into Mira, so that would leave you with Chris. Sounds great, except you know for a fact that Chris has a girlfriend already—a really popular girl at your school. But he is *so* gorgeous, and it seems like he's flirting with you. Do you dare?

You head to the movies with the guys. Go to 66.

You decide not to step in on Chris. Go to 68.

$\mathcal{W}$hen you and Mira walk into Polka Dots, you're blasted with loud music. "I love this place!" Mira says. "Let's look at the vintage jeans first." She heads over to that section. You follow her, but you've got your eye on the checkout counter, looking for Drew.

"Can I help you ladies with anything special today?" A tall guy with dark hair is standing next to you.

"Uh, hi," you answer. "Is Drew working today?"

"No, sorry, it's his day off. I'm Simon, though. If there's anything I can help you with, let me know," he says. He's dressed really cool, like he's in a band or something—black jeans, distressed black T-shirt, beat-up sneakers.

"We need dresses, for…" Mira pauses and looks over at you. "For a party we're going to."

"Cool." Simon smiles. "Follow me." As you walk behind him, you and Mira elbow each other and exchange a knowing look. This guy is yummy! Soon Simon has two or three dresses for each of you to try on, and he leads you over to the dressing room.

"This pink one is for you," he says, meeting your eyes as he hands you the hanger.

You try on the dress and come out. "I had a feeling that dress was going to be killer on you." Simon nods. "But I guess you could look great in anything, huh?"

You just look down, blushing and unsure of what to say. "I should probably change," you mumble, ducking back into the dressing room.

When you come back out, Mira scoots over to you and whispers, "He's into you! Go talk to him," and she gives you a little push in Simon's direction. You take the pink dress over to the counter where Simon is ringing someone else up. Maybe he does like you. But then again, maybe he just flirts with all the customers.

"I can ring you up over here," a girl standing behind the other register calls over to you. Do you wait for a turn to flirt more with Simon, or are you too shy?

65

You decide to stick with the girl's register. Go to 71.

You wait to talk to Simon some more. Go to 69.

"Let's go," Mira says, turning to you. "We'll have time to do our homework after—please?" she whispers, pulling a serious face.

"Okay," you say, smiling. "I'm in!"

"Cool!" Owen says, linking his arm through Mira's. "This way, ladies." He leads the way to the movie theater, leaving you and Chris to fall in step behind.

"So," Chris says, "I don't have any classes with you this year, do I?"

You shake your head, "No, but we had English together last year," you point out. That was when you first noticed him—and how utterly adorable he is!

"Right, I remember that. I remember you…," he says, glancing over at you. You look up into his brown eyes for a second and almost forget that he has a girlfriend. Why is he flirting with you when he's taken? Maybe things aren't going well with her…maybe they're breaking up or something…? Your mind is spinning with the possibilities.

When you get into the movie theater, Chris steps ahead of you in line and buys your ticket. "You can get mine next time," he says, smiling. So there's going to be a next time? This guy is obviously sending some strong signals that he's into you!

You file into the theater, and Owen picks a row. He sits with Mira next to him, and you sit by Chris. The four of you talk until the theater gets darks and the trailers come on. "Popcorn?" Chris whispers next to you, holding out the container.

"No, thanks," you whisper back.

"Drink?" he says next, holding up his soda.

"I'm good," you say, smiling.

"Kiss?" he asks, leaning in close to you. Before you can answer, you feel his lips touch your cheek, and you glance up to catch his eye. He reaches over to take your hand, and you...

67

Let him hold your hand. Go to 26.

Pull your hand away because he has a girlfriend. Go to 75.

"Come on, let's go!" Mira begs, looking you in the eye. "It'll be fun!"

"I would really like to, but I've got so much homework to do," you say. You're remembering that you blew off Kelly's planning meeting because you had too much work to do—what would she think if you just decided to go to a movie instead? She would definitely not be too happy!

"You can always do it later," Chris says, meeting your eyes.

"Or just do it on the bus on the way to school tomorrow morning," Owen laughs. "That's what I do!"

You shake your head. "Sorry, guys, you go on without me. Mira, I'll see you tomorrow, 'kay?"

"Okay." You can tell that Mira isn't happy with your choice, but she'll be okay—she's getting to go to a movie with her crush!

Go to 95.

"That's okay," you tell the other cashier. "I'll just wait."

"We know Simon," Mira adds. The girl just shrugs and gets busy fixing something behind the counter.

In a minute, it's your turn. When Simon sees you, his face lights up in a big smile. "So you're getting that pink dress? Good call; it looks great on you," he says while ringing you up. When you hand him the money, he takes your hand for a second and looks into your face. "Hey, how old are you, anyway…are you guys in high school?" he asks.

"How old do you think we are?" Mira flirts.

"I don't know," Simon answers, folding up the dress and sliding it into a bag. "Old enough to go on a date with me?" he asks, handing you the bag and meeting your eyes.

"Maybe" is all you can manage to say.

"Let me have your number and I'll call you sometime," he says, sliding a small piece of paper and a pen over the counter. "Let's go out."

You glance at Mira and she raises her eyebrows at you. Simon seems to think that you're older than you really are, so what do you do now?

You give him your number and play along. Go to 79.
You admit that you're too young for him. Go to 81.

"Okay," you say to the girl cashier, and move over to her register.

"Don't you want to talk to Simon?" Mira whispers to you. You shake your head.

"I just can't do it," you say, feeling shy.

Mira shrugs. "Your loss," she says.

When the cashier is done ringing you up, you grab your bag and head for the door.

"Hey, see ya!" Simon calls out. You turn and give him a quick wave, then open the door and scoot out to the sidewalk.

"I really do think he was into you," Mira giggles. "Remember when he said, 'If there's *anything* I can help you with...,' she says in a deep voice, imitating Simon.

"Oh stop!" you say, but can't help laughing.

"What's so funny?" a male voice behind you asks. You and Mira both spin around to see Owen and his friend Chris from school.

"I thought you guys had practice today." Mira's whole face lights up when she sees Owen.

"Canceled," Owen explains. "What are you ladies up to?"

"We were just checking out dresses for the dance," Mira says quickly.

"You're going with someone?" Owen asks, suddenly looking very serious.

"No, just…wishful thinking, I guess." Mira blushes.

"Well, we're going to the movies," Chris says, pointing across the street to the movie theater. "Hey, you should come with us," he adds, looking right into your eyes. "I've been wanting to hang out with you and never get a chance to at school." You look down, blushing.

72

Owen is a great-looking guy, but in your opinion, his friend Chris is totally irresistible—with shaggy blond curls and warm brown eyes. But he's also totally off-limits—he's been dating one of the most popular girls in school for over a year.

"Yeah, come with us!" Owen says to Mira, and she looks over at you pleadingly.

"What do you say?" Chris asks. It seems like he's into you, but you know he's seeing someone. So you …

Head to the movies. Go to 66.

Decide to say no to the movies. Go to 68.

"*A*ctually," you tell Tyler, "I might be wrong. Maybe Anna is single after all. In fact, I'm pretty sure she is, now that I think about it."

You can tell by the look on his face that he's clearly into her. He'll probably end up asking her to the dance—deeply depressing! But you have only a second to dwell on it before someone suddenly sits down in the chair next to you. It's your best guy friend, Eddie!

"Hey, what are you doing here?" you ask. You're so glad to see him and get your mind off of Tyler and Anna.

"You know how Kelly can be," he starts to explain. "She sort of forced me to join. I'm not even sure how it happened."

"Yeah," you agree with a laugh, "that's why I'm here, too!"

"Okay, you guys," Kelly cuts in, "let's talk about committees. We have three: music, refreshments, and decorating. It's time to start planning," she says.

Go to 20.

"*W*ell, I'm pretty sure she's got a boyfriend," you say. "In fact, I think he's this really great guy— she's really into him," you hear yourself say, and can hardly believe you're lying so much!

"Oh man," Tyler says, "what a bummer. Too bad there aren't any other hot girls here. This committee is going to be so lame." He shakes his head.

No other hot girls? *Ouch!*

END

74

If you want to try telling the truth, go back to 18.

"What's wrong?" Chris asks you when you pull your hand away from his.

"You have a girlfriend," you whisper back. "Sorry." You stand up and scoot over to another seat on the other side of Owen so that you don't have to sit by Chris anymore.

"You okay?" Mira leans over and asks you.

"Fine," you whisper back. But for the rest of the movie you feel uncomfortable. When the film is over, you all file outside.

"I loved that!" Mira chirps. "Hey, let's all go and grab something to eat!"

"I have to go," Chris says curtly, not meeting your eyes. "Let's head out, Owen."

"You sure?" Owen says. "Maybe just a quick bite somewhere?"

Chris just shakes his head. "I've wasted enough time already," he says, casting a cold glance in your direction. "Let's go."

"Okay," Owen says, looking puzzled. "I'll see you tomorrow at school," he says to Mira as they walk away. Chris doesn't even wave goodbye.

"What happened in there?" Mira asks as soon as they're gone.

"He's a total dog," you start, and tell Mira what happened when the lights went down.

"Ewwww, he's bad news!" she agrees. "But what about me and Owen? Do you think he's going to ask me to the dance—oh no! I still don't have a dress!" Mira suddenly realizes. "Let's hit a few more stores before we go home," she suggests.

"I have a *lot* of homework to do," you admit. "And it's getting late—I really need to get home."

"Oh come on, one more? Pretty please?" Mira begs.

76

You agree to keep shopping. Go to 86.

You need to go home and get to work. Go to 95.

It would be way too weird to hang out with both Drew and Simon—especially since you were just flirting with Simon a few minutes ago!

"I already sort of know Drew from school," you explain to Simon, "so you don't need to introduce us."

"Oh really?" Mira says sarcastically. She knows that you don't *really* know Drew at all!

"I mean, maybe we'll hang out sometime, but it doesn't need to be a setup or anything." You feel your face turning red. "Anyway, Mira, didn't you say you have a ton of homework tonight?"

"Uh, yeah," Mira says slowly, then catching on, she adds, "right—I've got a lot of homework, so we better go. Bye, Simon!" she says, grabbing your arm and racing you out the door.

"Bye," Simon calls after you, a puzzled look on his face.

"Can you imagine being set up on a date?" you say to Mira once you're safely out on the sidewalk.

"How embarrassing! Drew is so cool, and a setup is so dorky! He'd never go for it, anyway!"

"Maybe he would," Mira says. "You never know, and it would be a chance to get to know him."

"Well, it's too late now," you say. "I just couldn't do it."

"At least you got the perfect dress," she says, pointing to your bag from Polka Dots. "Now all you need is a date to the dance!"

"And someone to help me get all this homework done before school tomorrow," you add. "Let's get a move on before we miss the last bus home."

Go to 95.

That night, you're sitting around, trying to do your homework but really just staring at your cell phone, wishing it would ring. Finally you break down and call Mira.

"He hasn't called me yet. Do you really think he likes me?" you ask her.

"Calm down," she assures you. "He will call, he's just busy. Maybe he's still at work. And besides, he didn't say he was going to call you *tonight*, did he?"

"I guess you're right," you say, plopping down on your bed with a sigh. "I just can't stop thinking about him!"

Just then, your phone beeps. A private call! "Oh, this could be him!" you yell.

"Call me later!" Mira orders as you switch over to the other call.

"Hey, it's Simon," a guy's voice says.

"Oh, hi," you respond, trying to sound casual.

"You know what, a funny thing happened after you guys left the store today," he says.

"Yeah, what's that?" you ask.

"My friend Drew showed up. Do you know him?" Simon asks.

You're about to say yes, and then stop yourself...if Drew showed up and talked to Simon, then that means...

"Yeah, he mentioned that he knows you guys. From school. And not only that, but that you're a year younger than him. That's pretty funny, huh?" Simon asks, but you can tell he doesn't really think it's funny—he's angry!

"Look, Simon, I'm sorry if you—if I made you think I was older or—"

"Oh, just forget it, and do me a favor—shop somewhere else, okay?" he says, and you hear him hang up.

80

You look down at your phone and let out a sigh. Sure, you've learned your lesson, but he turned out to be a huge jerk, anyway!

END

If you want to rethink giving him your number, go back to 69.

You look down at the piece of paper Simon put in front of you and almost write down your number. But then you stop. "Actually," you say, looking up at him, "would it be a problem for you if I *was* still in high school?"

"Well, it would mean that you're way too young for me," Simon laughs. "What school do you guys go to?"

Mira answers him, and he nods. "Right, that's how you know Drew. He goes there, too."

"We *sort* of know him," Mira says, nudging you with her elbow.

"Just a little," you add. "Not really."

"I have an idea," Simon says, a sparkle suddenly in his eye. "Drew is single, and he was just telling me that he wanted to find someone to ask to this school dance that's coming up. You'd be perfect for him; you're totally his type!" he says, pointing at you.

"Me?" you ask. "Really? I...um..."

"Yeah, absolutely. We should all hang out sometime." Simon smiles. "Seriously."

It sounds like he wants to set you up with Drew—who you have a serious crush on already! It could be slightly weird (especially if Simon tells Drew that you and Mira were kind of flirting with him), but it could also be great. Do you want to do it?

You say yes to the setup. Go to 138.

You're just not that into being set up. Go to 77.

"I'm a little nervous to go on my own tonight," you explain to Mira as you walk back to the bus. "I wish you weren't busy!"

"Well, call Kelly. Maybe she'll want to go," Mira offers.

"There's a problem, though—I told Kelly I had too much homework to help her out with her dance planning meeting today after school," you explain. "Do you think she'd be mad if I call her up now and ask her if she can go to a show with me?"

"Hmmmmm," Mira says. "The only way to find out is to call her and ask her."

"I guess," you say. "Or I just have to go alone."

83

You decide to call Kelly. Go to 101.

You are brave enough to go alone. Go to 97.

After holding hands all through the movie (and even letting him kiss you a few times!), you go home that night feeling like you're floating on a cloud. You've got a boyfriend! Or you will—once he breaks up with his girlfriend.

You're getting ready for bed when your cell phone buzzes—you have a text message from Chris already!

Can't stop thinking about U! XXXOOO, Chris

You smile dreamily. Chris is amazing!

❧

The next day, you take forever picking out the perfect outfit. You want to look great when you see Chris.

"Cool shirt, and your hair—you look great!" Mira says, coming up to you at your locker at school. "Can you believe last night?" she asks.

"I know!" you whisper back. "I think we both have dates to the dance now!"

"I'm in love with Owen," Mira admits, blushing.

"And I got a text from Chris last night saying that

he couldn't stop thinking about me!" you confess.

"But what about his girlfriend—Amy? Is he telling her today?" Mira whispers.

You just shrug. "I guess so. He didn't really want to talk about her. Maybe he called her last night and got it over with," you say hopefully.

"Don't look now…," Mira says in a singsong voice, and you turn to see Chris coming down the hall.

"Hi." You meet his eyes for a second and give him a little wave. Then you notice that Amy is walking right beside him. Uh-oh!

He just gives you a nod—like he barely knows you!—and keeps walking.

"What's up with that?" Mira asks, looking puzzled.

85

"I guess he hasn't told her yet," you say, but you feel so hurt.

"Well, are you going to talk to him about it?" Mira asks you.

You look at her and think for a second. What should you do?

_____ ℓ _____

You're ready to confront Chris about his girlfriend. Go to 104.

You want to give him some more time to deal with it on

his own. Go to 107.

"Okay! But really just one more store, then I have to get home," you tell Mira.

"This one," Mira says, pulling you into a brightly lit store as you walk past. "They have the coolest dresses—no where else in town carries the brands they have in here." She steers you over to the section with dresses and skirts.

"Look at that blue one," you say, pointing to a fitted, short blue dress on a sale rack. "You have to try it on, and it's on sale!"

Mira goes over to the rack and starts riffling through the dresses. "This one, this one, and maybe this?" she says, holding up an off-white, floor-length gown.

You shake your head. "It's kind of...no."

She shrugs and puts it back, picking up a beautiful pink dress instead. "Oh, you have to try this one on. Pink is your color!"

"I already have a pink dress," you tell her.

"Just come in the dressing room with me," Mira says, shoving the pink dress at you. "Please?"

You sigh—"Okay"—and follow her into the changing rooms. You slip into the pink dress and look in the mirror. It's...amazing. The most stunning piece of clothing you've ever tried on. You step out of the dressing room to show Mira.

"Oh. Wow" is all Mira can say. "You are getting that. It's crazy hot on you!"

"It *is* a great dress," you admit, looking in the full-length mirror. You change back into your clothes, thinking about it, and decide that you'll buy it—you have to, right?

You meet Mira up at the front counter, where she's already waiting in line with her blue dress.

"Hi," Mira says to the blond girl standing in front of her. "Don't we know you from school?"

When she spins around, you see that it's Kristen—the most popular girl you can think of. She twirls a piece of her long hair around one finger and looks at Mira, then at you. "No, I don't think so," she says in a snide voice. Then her eyes land on your dress. "I'm getting that dress," she says quickly.

"Yeah, it's really great, right?" you say to her.

"On me it is," she says, meeting your eyes with a cold blue stare. "But I saw it first. And I'm wearing it to the dance. Understand?" she asks.

"Uh, what do you mean?" Mira asks her. "Just because you're getting that dress doesn't mean that she can't get it, too."

"Oh yes, it does. I'm not going to show up at the dance wearing the same dress as some...nobody," she sniffs. "So why don't you put it back. Now. Or you *will* be sorry," Kristen says, and turns around to lay her dress on the counter.

While the sales clerk rings her up, you whisper to Mira, "What should I do?"

"I don't know," Mira whispers back.

You decide to get the dress anyway. Go to 5.

You put it back because you're afraid of the popular girl.

Go to 111.

$\mathcal{I}$t takes you a few minutes to come up with just the right IM, but finally you write:

Thanks, Milo! IOU a pizza after school (2morrow?) & if U don't like pizza, guess I'll have 2 be your date 2 the dance!

When you're done writing it, you read it over a couple of times, take in a deep breath, and push the "send" button. Then you wait. And wait. Maybe Milo thinks you're lame? Just then, an IM pops up on the screen—it's him!

Sorry, have 2 go. Talk to U about dance 2morrow @ school.

That's all it says, but that's enough! You can't wait to see him tomorrow—this could be big!

∽∾

The next day at school, you're nervous to go to math class, but when you do walk in the door,

Milo's not even there yet. You take your seat and wait for him to show up. He walks in and sits down without even looking at you. That's okay—you remind yourself that he's a shy guy. Maybe he's more comfortable flirting over IM.

As the teacher starts talking, you can't help stealing glances at Milo. He's really adorable, but is he just too shy for you? He hasn't turned around to look at you once, or even acknowledged that you're alive today! You're starting to wonder if maybe that whole IM thing last night was just a dream you had.

"...And next week, we're going to be talking about the math and science fair," the teacher says. "You'll be working on teams for your projects, so think about who you'd like to be paired up with." You instantly look over to Milo, but see that he's busy talking to the guy sitting next to him. Are they going to be a team? You're starting to feel beyond depressed!

Finally, after what feels like an eternity, class is almost over. Now you have to decide—are you going to grab Milo after class and try to talk to him about the dance, or should you just leave it alone for now? Maybe you could ask him to sit with you at lunch or something?

You decide to draw out this shy guy. Go to 116.
You'd rather he come to you. Go to 114.

$\mathcal{F}$inally, you settle on just sending him a simple "thanks" IM. But then you think of something funny that you could say and type up a better note—offering to take him out after school for pizza in exchange for more homework help. When you're done rewriting the text, you sit and stare at the computer for a minute. Is it too flirty to send?

A few more minutes go by and he hasn't responded to your "thanks" note, so maybe he's off-line now? You read over your note again and again. But you just can't bring yourself to send it. And you know he's too shy to make the first move. You let out a big sigh and close the IM window, shutting down your computer for the night.

When you see Milo at school tomorrow, maybe he'll actually talk to you. Or you could try to talk to him. But you have a funny feeling that he's the sort of guy who's better over IM—at least in the beginning. You can't stop kicking yourself for not sending that note! Next time, you'll take a chance—you've got to be brave to get those shy boys to notice you!

END

Want to see what might happen if you send him a flirty IM?
Go back to 95.

$\mathcal{M}$ilo doesn't say anything about the dance, and you feel funny for bringing it up. It's on the tip of your tongue to say, "Hey, are you going?" but you find that you just can't say it. So you don't. Instead, it's silent at your lunch table for a few minutes. Then, when it looks like Milo is almost done with his sandwich, you finally manage to say something.

"So, you must really like math, huh?" you hear yourself say, then you feel really dumb.

Milo just shrugs. "I guess," he says shyly. Then he balls up his lunch bag to throw it away. "See you later," he says, and gets up to go.

"Yeah, later," you say quietly, watching him leave. Why didn't you ask him about the dance when you had the chance? Ugh! Now he'll never know how much you like him—and you still don't have a date to the dance!

END

If you'd like to redo the lunch conversation, go back to 116.

You start in on your math homework, but after about two minutes you're so confused you have no idea what you're doing. Did the teacher even go over this in class? You grab your student directory to find someone you can ask for help. There is this one guy, Milo, in your class who is incredibly smart—and he's also incredibly cute, but he's so quiet. You've never really talked to him before.

Staring at the computer screen, you finally get up the courage to send him an IM. If he's online, you can get some homework help. What's wrong with that? You feel yourself blushing a little as you write him a quick note and send it off. In less than a minute, an IM pops up on your screen from Milo.

I can help U, what do U need 2 know?

You write him back with your questions about the homework, and he's quick to respond. He makes it look so easy! What a great guy. You're about to send him a note to say "thanks" and then think that maybe you should take things one step further—maybe ask him to hang out sometime so you can thank him in person?

U rock! Thanks for the help—I get it now. Do U want 2...

Ugh, what can you say? "Want to hang out" sounds so lame. Maybe you should just thank him and skip the flirting. Do you dare to try for more?

You want to send a flirty note. Go to 89.
You're too shy to flirt over IM. Go to 92.

$\mathcal{W}$hen you walk into the coffee shop, you find yourself wishing that you had called Kelly and asked her to come with you. The place is crowded with kids from your high school and the local college, but nobody that you know. You're feeling so awkward—why did you ever say you would do this?

"Hey," you hear someone say, and turn around. "I didn't know you were into this band!" It's Stacy, a girl from your school.

"Oh hi!" you say back. "Actually, I've never heard them before, but I'm meeting someone here." It makes you feel proud to say that, for some reason.

"Who? Anyone I know?" she asks.

"Drew Abbott; he's a year older than us—" you start to say.

"He's so awesome!" Stacy interrupts. "You're lucky. Are you guys dating?"

Just then, you spot Simon from across the room; he's waving you over. "I've got to go, that's my friend," you say quickly.

"He's foxy, too!" Stacy says with a sigh.

Suddenly, the night is looking up—you're out with two really good-looking guys!

When you get over to Simon, you see Drew is standing right next to him. "Hey, I know you from school," Drew says, smiling. He seems happy to see you.

"Yeah, I was just shopping at Polka Dots today and Simon mentioned this show, so here I am!" you say, trying to sound casual.

"They're really good," Drew says.

"Who?" you ask quickly. "Polka Dots?"

Drew laughs, "No, the band!"

"Oh right." You smile at how silly you must sound.

Before you can talk anymore, the band starts playing, and Drew's right—they are pretty good. You start moving to the music with the rest of the crowd, catching Drew's eye every now and then with a smile. You've never stood this close to him before, or noticed just how blue his eyes are. When the band takes a break, you notice that Simon is nowhere to be found. "Let's go outside for a minute," Drew says, grabbing a couple of bottles of water for you both.

"So, I don't usually see you out at the local shows," Drew says when you get outside.

"Actually, I don't usually go to things like this on school nights," you explain.

He just nods. "You have a boyfriend or something?"

"No," you say quickly. "I have a lot of homework!"

Drew laughs. "I've seen you around school before. I guess I just never thought to talk to you, or I didn't have a reason to...." He looks down at his black Converse, then back up at you. His eyes are such an intense color, you feel like you have to look away fast. "But now that I know we're into the same kind of music, we should hang out."

You just nod. "Yeah, that would be great," you hear yourself say, then feel uncool. You start wondering if Drew knows this was a setup.

"What kind of music do you think they'll have at that school dance next weekend?" he asks you, taking a quick drink of his water.

"I don't know," you say. "My friend is running the dance committee, so I sort of have to go and act like I'm having fun, whatever they pick!"

"I have an idea," Drew says, leaning over to you.

"Let's go together. If it's lame, we can bail out early and hit this show on the other side of town that I heard about. What do you say?"

"I say yes!" you tell him.

"It's a date." He smiles. "Hey, the band is going back on. Wanna dance?" he asks you, taking your hand.

"Definitely!" You smile back. Looks like Simon was right about you—you *are* Drew's type, and he's totally your type, too. Plus now you've got a date to the dance!!

END

The second you get on the bus, you call Kelly from your cell. "Listen, I have a question," you start.

"Don't you even want to know how the meeting went?" she asks you.

"Oh, sure, how was it?" you ask.

"It went *so* great. A lot of people showed up, and we came up with this great idea for the theme…," she goes on, but you're only half listening because you're so anxious to tell her your news.

"Did you hear me?" Kelly says. "Hey, are you listening?"

"Yes," you lie. "What did you say?"

"I asked you if you thought that was a good theme idea? What do you think?"

"Yeah, it sounds really good," you say, even though you didn't hear what the theme was! "I have to ask you something—it's a long story, but there's this show tonight, and Drew is going to be there. Do you know who he is?"

"The short guy in our study hall?" Kelly asks.

"No, not him—he's tall, dark hair, blue eyes…"

"Oh, him!" Kelly says.

"Anyway, I'm going to this show tonight to hang out with him and I really need you to come with me," you beg.

Kelly is quiet for a minute, then she says, "I thought you had a lot of homework. Don't you have some book report due or something?"

"Yes," you tell her—and it's true. "But this is important."

"Oh, not like my meeting this afternoon—that was okay to blow off. And now you want me to come do something with you?" You can tell from her voice that she's not happy.

"Look, Kelly, I didn't mean it like that," you start to say. "Your meeting was important, too, it's just—"

"Don't bother trying to explain," Kelly cuts you off. "I get it. You don't care about the dance committee. Well, guess what? I don't care about your crush on what's-his-name!"

"Kelly, come on...," you say, but she's already hung up! You look out the window of the bus and think about what she said. You hate to admit it, but she's right to be mad at you, and you're really bummed. Now your best friend is angry, and you have no one to go to the show with. You're not even sure you want to go anymore! How did a day that was going so great end up turning out so bad?

END

If you want to rethink asking Kelly to the show, go back to 83.

$\mathcal{I}$n the middle of your next class, you get another text message from Chris.

U look so cute 2day. ☺

Okay, so he's obviously into you. But then why was he acting so weird this morning? You decide that the next time you see him, you're going to ask him what's up. When you do run into him at lunch, though, he's with his girlfriend again!

"They don't look so unhappy," Mira points out, taking a bite of her sandwich.

"Yeah," your friend Kelly adds. "Are you sure he said he was going to break up with her?"

You look over at their table and see them sitting close together. Is he actually holding her hand?

"What are you going to do?" Kelly asks you.

"I guess I'm going to have to ask him about it," you say.

You get your chance before last period, when you see Chris by his locker—alone.

"Hi," you say quietly, sliding up next to him.

He's a little startled. "Oh, hey, how are you?" He smiles, but you can tell he's looking around behind you, probably checking to make sure his girlfriend doesn't see you together!

"How's it going with Amy?" you ask him. "I saw you with her at lunch."

"Yeah, that...," he says, looking in his locker for something. "Um...we're, um, working on stuff," he finally says.

"Uh-huh," you say. "Do you think you're still going to be 'working on stuff' the weekend of the school dance?"

"I don't know." Chris shrugs, looking at you. "You're too cute when you get mad, you know that?" He grins, running his fingers down your arm.

You pull your arm back. "Look, I'm not kidding around. If you're taking her to the dance, I want to know now," you say.

"You girls and that stupid dance," he says, closing his locker. "Is it really that important?" He leans his head against the locker door, his eyes level with yours. "I want to kiss you so bad," he whispers, "but I guess we can't do that here, huh?"

You look into his eyes and realize that you want to kiss him, too, even though you're not sure you can trust him.

What is *up* with this guy? He's obviously into you, but it looks like he wants to keep his girlfriend, too! Is he just playing with you? Maybe he really is about to break up with her and give you a chance. You're so confused!

You decide to forget about him and move on. Go to 122.

You want to wait it out and see what he does. Go to 129.

hat night when you get home, you check your e-mail and find a note from Chris.

Thinking about you all day. ♥

Adorable! He's the real thing. You're so glad you didn't bother him about his girlfriend stuff today—you're sure he'll deal with it when he's ready. And then you'll be able to go to the dance together! You can't wait.

The next day at school, you're looking all over the place, hoping to find Chris, even if it's just to see him for a second. But when you finally do run into him, he's with Amy, walking in the hall between classes. "Hi," you say as he walks by, but this time he doesn't even acknowledge you. Obviously, he hasn't broken up with her yet.

"So what's up with you and your secret agent lover man?" Kelly jokes in study hall. "Did he ask you to the dance yet?"

"Not exactly," you say sadly. "He sent me a cute

e-mail, and this text message…." You show her your phone.

"'You = Hot,'" she reads out loud, looking at the message. "Uh…okay. But what's up with his girlfriend?"

You shrug. "I don't know, he keeps sending me all these messages and e-mails like he's into me, but when I see him in the halls, he's always with her and he acts like he doesn't know me!"

"What are you going to do?" Kelly asks.

108

You decide it's time to talk to Chris about his girlfriend.

Go to 104.

You still trust him and want to wait. Go to 129.

$\mathcal{A}$fter school, you're one of the first to show up for the meeting. There are two girls there who you know from gym class, and one guy you've never seen before who's not really your type. Things are looking grim. Then you hear the door swing open behind you and turn around, expecting to see Kelly, but instead, the cute guy from your study hall is standing right there in front of you!

"Is this the dance committee meeting?" he asks you.

Looking into his dark green eyes, you find yourself unable to speak. "Uh, yeah, yes, this is it," you finally manage to say. You quickly grab a seat, and he takes the one next to you.

"I'm Tyler," he says, leaning over to glance at you. "You're in my study hall, right?"

So he *has* noticed that you're alive! You feel yourself grinning. "Yeah, hi," you say, and tell him your name, in case he doesn't know it.

Just then, Kelly walks in with another guy—you recognize him from the football team. He's really tall with dark red hair—definitely a hottie. Maybe Kelly was right—this could be the perfect way to meet your date to the dance.

"Okay, let's get started," Kelly says, looking around at everyone in the room. "We have a lot of work to do, but first we need to come up with a theme. I was thinking 'Under the Sea'—we can decorate the gym to look like an underwater scene, complete with fish and mermaids and everything."

Beside you, Tyler lets out a groan. "Sorry, but that sounds lame. Didn't they just do that two years ago? Let's come up with something cooler." A couple of kids nod in approval, but you can tell from looking at Kelly's face that she's hurt. So far this meeting isn't going well. She meets your eyes and asks you, point-blank, "What do you think of the 'Under the Sea' theme? Do you think it's 'lame' too?"

You don't want to hurt Kelly's feelings, but Tyler does have a point. Do you support your best friend or side with Tyler?

You decide to support Kelly. Go to 9.

You side with Tyler. Go to 11.

When you get home that night, you're regretting your choice. You're so bummed that you won't get to wear that amazing dress. You look through your closet for something else to wear and try on the only other pink dress you own—the vintage one you just bought. When you tried it on, it looked great, but now it looks so dull and boring compared to that perfect dress.

You sit on your bed and let out a sigh. You feel so discouraged about going to the dance now if it means that you have to see Kristen wearing *your* dress. Then you suddenly get an idea…. You jump up and try on the vintage dress again, then grab your wide black belt and cinch it low around your hips, glancing in the mirror. That looks sort of cool. Now maybe if it didn't have these cap sleeves and it were strapless…? You find a sewing kit and get to work making this dress the dress of your dreams!

☙

Before you know it, it's the night of the dance. Mira and Kelly come over to your house so you can all get ready together. "So, let's see this dress you've been working on forever," Mira says, peeking into your closet. You pull out the dress and dash into the bathroom.

"Give me two minutes!" you say, slipping into the dress. When you walk back into your bedroom, both Kelly and Mira gasp. "You look amazing!" Mira screams. "I'm in love with this!" She lightly touches the lace trim you sewed onto the top. "How did you do it? You are a born designer!"

Kelly just stands there looking at you. "What do you think?" you finally ask her.

"Um, well, the belt is sort of ... big. And I'm not sure I love all those little flowers you sewed all over the skirt part," she says. You can tell from her face that the dress just isn't her style.

"You hate it," you say. "It's okay. You can tell me!"

"I don't hate it, but I don't know if you should wear that to the dance. I mean, it *is* a little out there," Kelly says. "Right?"

Mira shakes her head. "You're wrong. I think it's

the best dress I've ever seen. And it looks stunning
on you. You must, must, *must* wear this!" she says,
clapping.

What do you do?

You decide to wear the dress you created. Go to 118.
You'd rather wear something simpler. Go to 120.

When math class ends, you make sure to walk out right next to Milo—putting yourself in his line of vision so that he actually sees you. After all, he *did* say that he would talk to you about the dance today at school. But even when you walk out of the class practically touching his hand, he acts like you don't exist.

Later that day, you see him at lunch and try to make eye contact, but he looks away. What's up? Is he really that shy? What about the dance? You're dying to know if he's going with someone.

At the end of the day, you walk by his locker, and you hope that he sees you, but he's not there. So you circle around and walk back by his locker again. Still no luck. You can't stand it! Finally, you go out to the curb where the buses line up and sit on a bench to wait for him. Yes, you'll look obvious, but you just don't care anymore.

When he does come out of the school, he's walking alone—here's your chance! You rush over to him before he can climb onto his bus. "Hey,

Milo," you manage to say as he reaches the door. "I just wanted to tell you, um…"

"Let's go," the bus driver yells. "Are you in or not?" He looks at Milo.

"Um…well…thanks, again, for the help. With the math," you mumble.

"No problem," Milo says, unable to meet your eyes. He climbs up the stairs onto the bus. The driver gives you a scowl as he slams the door shut and puts the bus into gear. As they drive away, you realize that you've waited so long for Milo that you actually missed your own bus ride home—and you burst into tears.

Why did he say he was going to talk to you about the dance and then not even look at you all day? Is he just shy or does he not like you? It's driving you crazy, and now you'll never now. You wish you had asked him when you had the chance!

END

If you want to ask Milo what's up, go back to 89.

$\mathcal{W}$hen class is over, you make your way to the door at the same time as Milo.

"Hey, thanks again for helping me last night. I was so lost!" you tell him.

He looks down shyly. "No problem, really, I don't mind," he says. Standing this close, you can't help but wonder what he would look like without his glasses. "Anytime you need help with math or with science homework, I'm pretty good at both, so you can always ask me," he says.

"Thanks," you start to say, and then you get a great idea. "Actually, there is this thing in chemistry class that I just don't understand. Maybe I could sit with you at lunch and we could talk about it?"

"Sure." Milo grins. "I'm going to lunch right now."

You walk into the lunchroom together and sit down. "Oops," you say, feeling really dumb. "I can't believe this—I forgot my chemistry book!"

"Oh," Milo says, taking a bite of his sandwich. "That's okay, you can e-mail me tonight if you remember the question."

You both sit there silently for a few minutes, eating. He's really hard to talk to! You suddenly remember the IM you sent him last night, about the dance, and feel your face starting to turn red, just at the memory!

"You know, my friend Kelly is heading up the dance committee this year," you say, hoping that will make it easier to bring up the dance.

"Oh yeah?" Milo nods, but then he's quiet again. He seems to like you—after all, he *is* sitting with you. And he's such a cutie! Do you dare ask him if he has a date to the dance?

117

You ask him about the dance. Go to 136.
You're too shy. Go to 94.

You turn and look at yourself in the mirror. The dress is unusual—true. But you feel great in it. And one thing's for sure, no one else will have one like it!

"I'm going to wear it!" you say, and slip into your white heels.

"Of course you are!" Mira says. "Now sit and let me do your eye makeup," she orders.

Kelly shrugs. "It's your dress, so it's your choice," she says. "Where's your hair dryer?"

In half an hour, the three of you look amazing, and you're ready to go. Kelly's dad gives you all a ride to the dance and drops you off outside. As you're walking into the gym, you stop for a minute and adjust your belt. "I don't know," you say, looking down at the dress. "Maybe this is a mistake?" The dress is pretty funky, and you're starting to doubt yourself.

Mira grabs your arm. "Come on!" she says, pulling you. "You look fabulous and I'm proud to be seen with you. Let's go in there!"

You turn to Kelly, walking behind you. "Actually," she says, "I've gotten kind of used to it now, and I like it, too," she admits. "It doesn't really matter what you're wearing, you look great in anything!"

You give Kelly a big smile—she always knows just what to say.

Go to 125.

You turn and look at yourself in the mirror. "Maybe it is too much," you say, running your hands over the wide black belt. "I don't know...."

"Here," Kelly says, looking in your closet. "Wear this little black minidress; it always looks great on you."

"I still think you should wear the one you made," Mira says. "But it's up to you—you have to feel comfortable."

"Right," you say, taking the black dress into the bathroom and changing quickly into it. It's a simple dress, but Kelly's right—it does look good on you. "Better?" you say, doing a spin in the black dress for your friends.

"Much better," Kelly says. "Now let's do something with your hair. Sit," she orders.

"And I'll do your eye makeup," Mira says, leaning over you. "When I'm done with you, no one is going to even bother to notice what you're wearing!"

You have to laugh. You feel so lucky to have such good friends. When all three of you are ready, you stand in front of the mirror. Kelly in her scarlet dress and black shoes, Mira in the bright blue dress that looks so great on her, and then you. "I feel like this dress is so...boring," you say. "I don't know, maybe I should wear the other one." You look over at the funky pink dress now lying on your bed.

"Well, whatever you're doing, you better do it fast, my dad will be here to pick us up in about two minutes!" Kelly says.

You pick up the pink dress and look at it one more time, then decide to...

121

Wear the funky pink dress that you made. Go to 125.
Stay in the black dress. Go to 139.

The night of the dance, Mira and Kelly come over to help you get ready. You can't help but feel a bit sad about Chris—you really would have liked to go to the dance with him, but you know you made the right decision.

"He's just bad news," Mira points out as she's putting your eye shadow on.

"I know, but I liked him, and I thought he liked me," you say, tearing up.

"No crying! I'm trying to do your eyeliner here!" Mira laughs. "And no crying over that loser, period!"

Kelly puts down the curling iron for a second. "You know, he's probably going to be there tonight—with her," she points out, spraying her updo with hairspray.

"Kelly's right," Mira says. "But who cares? When I get done with this face, you're going to look so amazing, and he's going to be one sorry sucker!"

You have to laugh—you're so lucky to have two great best friends.

By the time you get to the dance, you're still feeling pretty good. That is, until you see him. With her.

"I don't know if I can take this," you say to Mira.

"I guess no amount of makeup can cover up a broken heart, huh?" she asks.

You feel like you're about to start crying, and Mira picks up on your mood. She takes your arm to lead you to the girls' bathroom so you won't make a total fool out of yourself. But as you cross the floor, someone comes up beside you. It's Ralph, a guy from your English class. "Hi, wow, you look great, how are you? I'm so glad you came to the dance!" He's talking really fast and trailing alongside you as you walk. "So, uh, I was wondering if maybe you wanted to dance? I mean, if you're busy, that's cool, but if you want to dance, maybe you want to dance with me? If you don't, it's okay," he says, all in one breath.

You and Mira both stop to look at this boy. You've known Ralph for years—and he's just not your type. He's nice, but you've never really thought about him as a "guy" at all. He's just ... Ralph.

But now—you look up and see that Chris has

spotted you. Maybe you should take Ralph up on his offer and dance with him, just to see how Chris likes that!

You decide to dance with Ralph. Go to 143.
You'd rather just hang out with your friends. Go to 146.

$\mathcal{W}$hen you walk into the dance, you forget all about your dress problems for a second—because you can't believe all the work Kelly has done to decorate the gym with the underwater theme.

"Kelly! You did a great job—look at this place, I don't even recognize it!" you exclaim.

Kelly blushes a little, almost matching her scarlet dress. "Whatever, it's not a big deal," she says bashfully.

Just then the music kicks in and Mira grabs both of you. "Dance. Now," she orders, pulling you onto the dance floor. The music is amazing, and you find yourself dancing to the next song—and the next.

"Cool dress," you hear someone say. It's a senior guy you've never talked to before who's dancing next to you.

"Thanks," you say quickly.

"Yeah, I love it!" his date says. She's also a senior, and really pretty. "I saw you when you walked in. Where did you get that?"

"I sort of made it," you explain.

"Wow, it's killer!" the girl says as they dance off.

You're feeling pretty good about the dress, too, even though you have gotten a couple of weird looks from some people. You scoot over to the refreshment table to grab a drink after dancing to another song, and you're getting a soda for Mira, too, when you hear a voice say, "Ugh, what are you wearing? What *is* that?" It's Kristen. She's wearing that amazing dress, and you hate to admit it, but it does look great on her.

"Yeah, where did you get that dress?" Kristen's friend Dani asks you.

"I made it," you say proudly, trying to walk past them and get back to the dance floor.

"It's great!" you hear Dani say, and you spin around.

"What?!" Kristen yells. "It's horrible, how can you say that?" she practically yells at Dani.

"Sorry, Kristen," Dani says. "But I like it. In fact, I think her dress is even better than yours!"

Kristen stares daggers at Dani for a second, then lets out a huff and storms off.

"Thanks," you say quietly to Dani as you make your way back to Mira and Kelly.

"And now we are ready to announce the King

and Queen of the Sea!" The principal is up onstage, ready with two golden crowns. You hand Mira her drink and watch to see who will win. "Gee, I wonder if it's going to be Kristen...again," Mira whispers to you sarcastically, and you have to giggle. She *does* always win everything.

Suddenly the room gets quiet. You're in the middle of swallowing a drink of soda when you feel everyone looking at you. "What?" you turn to Mira and say. "What's wrong?"

"He just called your name—you're the queen, silly!" she says.

"Go up there and get your crown!" Kelly claps and jumps up and down.

You hand Mira your drink as if you're in a trance. Queen of the Sea—You?! It's impossible! You weave through the crowd to get to the stage, and you can hear people commenting on your dress.

"I heard she made it," one girl says. "It's so cool!" a guy says.

You make your way up to the stage and walk by Kristen, who had been waiting by the stairs, probably so sure her name was about to be called. She stares at you for a second, and gives you a snarky look. As you scoot by her and go up to get your crown, you just smile at her and say, under your breath, "Nice dress."

END

You decide to try to be patient, since Chris really does seem to be the guy of your dreams. But you still can't believe that he tried to kiss you at school—especially since he still hasn't broken up with Amy! He's crazy...or maybe he's just crazy about you. You know it's wrong, but thinking about him gives you butterflies. You just can't help it. But then there's the problem of who he's taking to the dance. If he doesn't break up with Amy soon, what are you going to do?

That afternoon, you get an e-mail from him. You feel your heart beat fast when you click it open.

Missing you. Why didn't I kiss you today when I had the chance? ☺

He's adorable! You don't care what anyone else says about him. He just gets you! You click on "reply" and decide it's time to ask him about the dance.

Maybe you can kiss me at the dance. Are we going together?

You click "send" before you can think too hard about it and doubt yourself. Why not put your real feelings out there?

You wait for a response for a few minutes, but don't get one. Pretty soon, it's time to eat dinner, but you're dying to know what he's going to say back. Finally, right before bedtime, you get an e-mail.

Sorry, not going to the dance with anyone. ☹

You sigh. He's probably too upset about breaking up with Amy to go out on a date to the big school dance just yet. But that's okay with you—you're willing to wait for him. Now the only question is, do you want to go to the dance without him, or should you just stay home, too?

You decide to go to the dance alone. Go to 148.

You'd rather just stay home than be without Chris. Go to 151.

"Mr. Marshall, this is going to take forever! I really can't move at all," you explain, pointing at your legs wrapped up tight in the mermaid suit.

"Oh, I see what you mean," Mr. Marshall says, looking down at your feet sticking out of the bottom of the tight costume.

You're just about to open your mouth and ask him if maybe he could carry you when he says, "Oh look, there's a little hook right here." He points to your ankle, where there is a small metal clasp.

You lean down and undo it, opening the bottom part of the costume so that you can walk easily. "I guess I didn't see that," you say, feeling your face turn bright red.

"Let's head out, Ms. Mermaid, your audience awaits," Mr. Marshall says with a bow. You love the way he talks—there's something about him that's just so adorable!

When the two of you walk out into the parking lot, you feel everyone's eyes on you—or maybe it's just in your imagination. But it sure feels like everyone is staring at you in the costume. You cut through all the other fund-raising tables and head straight to the dunking booth, which is being filled with water.

"Well, up in the booth, young lady," Mr. Marshall says to you, holding your arm to steady you as you climb into the booth. You sit on the bench and look out over the parking lot. There are a few guys already waiting in line to try to dunk you, but you're not nervous.

"You all set?" Mr. Marshall says before closing up the booth with you inside.

"Almost," you say, rehooking the clasp on your mermaid fin so that it hangs down and covers your feet. "Don't you think mermaids are so romantic?" you hear yourself say, and wonder why that just popped out of your mouth.

"Oh, I don't know," Mr. Marshall laughs. "They're fish. That's not especially romantic." The puzzled look on his face makes you realize that he's not interested in flirting with you at all. *Oops!*

As he turns to go down the stairs, someone throws out the first ball at the target—and it hits dead on! The next thing you know, you're splashing down into the tank of cold water. When you stand up to climb back onto the bench, you realize that you forgot to put on waterproof makeup this morning, and mascara is running all over your face! You sit back up on the booth seat and look out over the crowd. Everyone is having a good laugh at you, including Mr. Marshall. Suddenly, this whole fund-raising thing seems like a very bad idea. How could you have ever thought you had a chance with a *teacher*?

One thing is for sure, you're very popular—the line to "dunk the mermaid" is growing by the minute. Too bad there aren't many guys at school who want to take a drenched mermaid to the dance....

133

END

If you want to rethink flirting with the teacher, go back to 51.

The night of the dance, Mira and Kelly come over to help you get ready. When you slip into the fantastic pink dress, they both stand back and look at you.

"I'm so glad you're wearing it, and that you didn't let Kristen scare you!" Kelly says.

"You look stunning! There is no way Kristen can look half as good as you do!" Mira says. "But we do need to do something with your face," she jokes.

"And your hair needs some help," Kelly laughs, picking up the curling iron.

An hour later, Mira has done your eye shadow, liner, and blush while Kelly has worked wonders with your hair. When you look in the mirror, you almost can't believe what you see. "Is that me?" you say, staring at the pretty girl reflected there.

"Let's go show Kristen the competition!" Mira says.

When you walk into the gym, you immediately feel everyone's eyes on you. Are they all shocked that you're wearing the same dress as Kristen, or do they just think you look amazing?

"Wow," one guy says, coming over to you. "Uh, do I know you? I'm Josh," he says. "Do you want to dance?"

"She's with us," Mira laughs, pulling you away from him. "Hello, beautiful," another guy says as you walk past. You've never felt this pretty in your whole life—maybe the dress is magic or something?

"I thought I warned you!" you hear a voice say, and turn to see Kristen, just as she throws a glass of red punch in your face!

"*Ahhhhhh!*" you scream, wiping the dripping punch from your eyes.

"Here," Mira says, blotting your face with a napkin. Kelly quickly catches any drips before they hit your dress.

135

"Are you crazy?" you turn to Kristen and say. "It's just a stupid dress!"

"It's not just a dress—it's MY dress," Kristen says, "and I told you not to wear it." She reaches out to grab your dress and almost tears it! You can't believe things have gotten to this point. How should you react?

You fight back. Go to 154.

You'd rather walk away from her. Go to 156.

"*A*nyway," you go on, feeling awkward, "the dance is going to be amazing this year with her in charge. She's really organized and she has all these great ideas, and I'm really looking forward to it and everything...." You can tell you're rambling, but you don't know how to stop yourself. You wish Milo would just say something already!

"That's cool," he says, and then opens his bag of chips and starts munching on them, smiling at you.

"Yeah, so, school dances and all that. What do you think about the dance? I mean, you know, this dance? Do you think you might go, or not go, or maybe you haven't thought about it at all...." You trail off, waiting for him to say something, but instead he just gives you a grin and laughs a little.

"What's so funny?" you ask.

"I like that you get nervous, too," he says shyly. "Whenever I see you, I always think that since you're so beautiful, you must be someone who's really confident, but I like how you can be shy, too." He looks at you and meets your eyes for a second.

136

Suddenly, you feel like you're the only two people in the lunchroom. "I guess what I'm trying to say is that I like you. I like how you are—with me."

"Oh" is all you can manage to say. You look down at your lunch.

"And I *have* thought about the dance. After you sent me that IM last night, I realized that I would like to go," he says, reaching over to take your hand, "with you."

You look up into his eyes, feeling so happy that you took a chance on the shy guy. Because now you have a date to the dance!

END

"I'd love to hang out with you and Drew sometime," you tell Simon.

"Cool," he says, grinning. "Listen, there's a show tonight—this band we really like is playing at the coffee shop. You should come—and you can come, too," he says, looking at Mira.

"I'm busy tonight," Mira says. "Dinner with my dad," she explains, turning to you. "But you should go."

"I don't know, it's getting late. I've got piles of homework, my book report is due...," you say.

Mira leans in and whispers to you, "Oh come on, this is your big chance for a date to the dance!" She giggles.

Simon raises his eyebrows at you both. "What's so funny?"

"Nothing," you say quickly.

"So are you in or what?" he says with a smile.

You look over at Mira, then back at Simon, and decide to...

Hang with Simon and Drew. Go to 83.

Head home to do your homework. Go to 95.

$\mathcal{L}$ooking at the dress again, you decide it's just too much for you. "I guess I'll just wear this black dress," you tell the girls, "but it does feel a little boring."

"You look great," Kelly says.

"Don't worry about it," Mira agrees. "We're going to have so much fun, no matter what you decide to wear!"

When you get to the dance, the gym looks amazing. "Kelly, I can't believe how much work you did," you say, turning to your friend. She blushes a red that matches her scarlet dress.

"It's not that big a deal," she says quietly.

As the music kicks in, Mira grabs your arm. "Let's dance!" she yells, and you all head for the dance floor. And that's when you see her—Kristen, wearing the perfect dress that you had wanted to wear. And she looks stunning, with her blond hair in an updo, dangling silver earrings, and beautiful silver shoes.

"Oh," you hear Mira say next to you.

"She almost looks like a fairy-tale princess," Kelly says with a sigh.

Before you can say anything, you look down at your boring black dress and feel the tears forming in your eyes—suddenly you're crying. Why do the popular girls always get their way? Life is so unfair sometimes! You run to the girls' bathroom, where you can sob in peace. Even though you just got to the dance, you already want to go home. Your night is ruined.

END

140

If you'd like to rethink what you're wearing to the dance, go back to 120.
If you'd like to rethink what you're wearing to the dance, go back to 120.

The night of the dance, Eddie shows up at your house in a rented limousine. You can't believe he would go to the all that trouble, especially since you two are already good friends—he doesn't have to prove anything to you!

"You really didn't have to do all this," you tell him when he hands you flowers in the car. "Really, it's…" You look around the inside of the fancy limo and sigh. "It's too much!" You smile.

"It's not too much," Eddie says, looking at you. His eyes are sparkling—you've never seen him so happy. "I want you to have the best night ever tonight."

You're glowing. How did you get so lucky?

When you get to the dance, you meet up with Mira and Kelly and their dates and you all hit the dance floor right away.

"Where's Eddie?" You suddenly realize he's not next to you anymore.

"He was just here," Mira says, looking around.

Then you see him crossing the dance floor,

holding drinks for everyone. He catches your eye with a grin. He's always been such a good friend, and now you can tell he's going to be the most amazing boyfriend!

When your group takes a break from dancing, Mira's date, Owen, says, "There's a big party over at the hotel after this." He nudges Mira as he's talking. "We're going; you guys should come, too." He looks at you and Eddie.

"What kind of party?" you ask.

"You know, the football team, some guys from school," Owen explains. "Tim's older brother is bringing beer!" Owen lets out a big hoot and puts his arm around Mira. She just smiles up at him—obviously, she's totally in love.

"Will you guys come?" Mira asks you. "I really want you to."

You look over at Eddie and decide…

To hit the after-party. Go to 160.

That an after-party is not your scene. Go to 162.

"Okay, Ralph, sure, I'll dance with you," you say, never taking your eyes off of Chris across the room. As you move to the dance floor, you can see that Chris is totally shocked—he probably thinks you're there with Ralph, and that you got over him super fast.

As soon as you start moving to the music, you realize your mistake—Ralph is the worst dancer ever! And you're about to be the laughingstock of the whole school if you don't do something quick. Before Ralph can embarrass you with any more of his wacky moves, you reach up and throw your arms around his neck, pulling him close to you—even though it's not a slow song. "Kiss me," you whisper to him. "Now!" you order, as you see Chris watching you both.

"What?" Ralph says, shocked. You pull his face down to yours and force your lips onto his. It's not the most romantic kiss ever, but from across the room, it probably looks convincing. Ralph shuts his eyes and just stands there like a statue the whole time—even once you stop kissing.

"Ralph, you okay?" you ask him. "Hey, Ralph?"

"That was the most amazing thing that has ever happened to me," he says, opening his eyes. Just then, you see Chris walking up behind him.

"What do you think you're doing?" he says to Ralph, grabbing him by the shoulder and spinning him around.

"Huh?" Ralph is totally confused.

"Keep your hands—and your mouth—off my girl!" Chris yells, and then punches poor Ralph straight in the nose!

"Oh no—" you start to say, but before you can do anything, Ralph jumps on Chris, and the two of them are on the ground in an instant, punching and hitting each other while a crowd forms around them.

"What's going on?" Owen, Chris's best friend, runs over. "Hey!" he yells as he tries to pull Ralph off of Chris.

"No way you football guys are ganging up on him!" Ralph's nerdy friend, Clyde, says as he jumps on Owen's back. "Leave him alone, you jerks!" Clyde yells.

You stand back in shock as the fight escalates. Suddenly all the nerds and football players in the school are hitting each other—it's a huge brawl! When the chaperones finally break it up a few minutes later, you see that Ralph has a bloody nose, and Chris's eye is swelling and purple. You just wanted to make Chris a tiny bit jealous, not cause a huge fight!

The principal quickly takes the stage and grabs the microphone. "The dance is over! Everyone go home, now! I will not tolerate fighting on school grounds! Anyone who was caught fighting tonight gets an automatic three-day suspension," he announces. "That's it, everyone out, now. This will be the first and LAST dance this year, thanks to your childish behavior."

So much for making Chris a *little* jealous!

145

END

If you want to rethink your plan to get back at Chris,
go back to 122.

"You know what, Ralph," you say, "I was just going to the bathroom, so maybe when I get back, okay?" That's a nice way to let him down easy.

"Yeah, okay, great, maybe later!" Ralph says, and you can tell that you made his night.

"Don't look now, but we've been spotted," Mira says, looking over at Chris. "He's staring at you."

"I guess he didn't think I would be brave enough to come by myself, after how he treated me," you say.

"But you *are* brave enough," Mira points out. "Do you still need to go in the bathroom for a good cry, or are you feeling better?" she asks.

"I'm good," you say quickly, glancing over at Chris. "I really am."

"Then let's have fun!" Mira smiles and pulls you onto the dance floor. "Let's dance!" You feel Chris's eyes watching as you and Mira start moving to the music, and it makes you self-conscious for a second.

"Hello, gorgeous girls!" you hear someone say next to you—it's your best guy friend, Eddie!

"Hey, handsome!" you say.

"You look amazing!" Mira shouts—and he does, in cool jeans and a vintage jacket over a T-shirt.

"Good enough to dance with you two?" Eddie asks, and joins you on the dance floor.

"There you guys are!" Kelly says, joining your group. "I just got cornered by Ralph over there—he's looking for you!" she says, pointing at you with a grin.

"A popular lady tonight," Eddie laughs. You dance and twirl on the floor, grabbing Kelly's and Mira's hands, giggling. You look over to where Chris is standing, still watching you, and suddenly you just don't care. Your real friends are here with you, and you're so lucky to have them. The right guy will come along when the time is right—but for tonight, you're just going to have fun!

147

END

The night of the dance, Mira and Kelly come over to help you get ready. "I don't even know why I'm going," you grumble while Mira is doing your eye makeup. "I only want to see Chris!"

"I heard that he and Amy still haven't broken up," Kelly says, "so I don't think you should be so into him just yet."

"She's right," Mira says, adding some smoky eyeliner to your upper lids. "I don't know about Chris. I mean, I know you like him, but I just don't trust the guy."

"Really?" you say, opening your eyes and taking a look in the mirror. Mira has done a great job again. "Thanks, Mira, that looks so perfect. I only wish Chris was going to be there tonight to see me," you say sadly.

"Oh boy." Mira sighs. "Are you hearing us at all?"

"I hear you, it's just that you guys don't know him the way I know him," you explain. "He's about to break up with her. And he wants to be with me. That's all there is to it."

"So why isn't he going to the dance with you?" Kelly asks, taking the hot rollers out of her long hair.

"Because...," you say, pausing to think. "It's just too soon for something like that. It would kill his ex-girlfriend. Besides, I just got a text message from him today," you say, snatching up your phone. "See," you say, showing them the readout. "It says, 'Wish I could see you right now.' That's just so him, so sweet," you say.

Just then, a car honks outside. "That's my dad, here to pick us up, let's go!" Kelly says.

When you get to the dance, you're still feeling a bit blue. You decide to text Chris a message telling him how much you miss him, just so he'll know that you're thinking of him.

"Come on, let's dance!" Kelly says, grabbing your arm and forcing you to put down your phone.

"Okay," you say, and head for the dance floor...and that's when you see Chris! He looks adorable dressed up, and you feel your heart skip a beat. You can't believe he came here tonight—how did he know you were going to be here? You didn't tell him you were going on your own. Your mind is racing, and you feel your feet taking you straight over to him as if you're walking on a cloud.

"Chris!" you say, locking eyes with him.

"Oh, hey," he says, looking confused. "I…uh… I thought you weren't coming tonight…," he mumbles.

"Yeah, how did you find out I was going to be here?" you say quickly.

"Hi," you hear someone say—it's Amy! What's she doing here? She moves in next to Chris and links arms with him. "Who's this?" she says, looking at you snottily.

"Oh, this is someone I know from, um, a class I have," Chris starts to say.

"I'm Amy," she says, "Chris's *girlfriend*." She smiles at you and you suddenly feel like you're going to pass out. He never broke up with her—he never even had any plans to! They're here together!

You race from the dance floor, barely able to hold back the tears. How could he do that to you? How could you have fallen for such a jerk? Your night at the dance has ended—with a broken heart.

150

END

If you want to forget about trying to start a relationship with Chris, go back to 104.

$\mathcal{Y}$ou look at Chris's e-mail and feel totally bummed. But he's obviously going through so much right now, and you just want to be there for him. You write him back a quick note.

Then I won't go to the dance either. Thinking of you! XOXOXO.

And you mean it—if you can't go with him, you'd rather not go at all.

❧

"Come on," your friend Mira says on the night of the dance. "Just come with me and Kelly; we'll have a blast, just the three of us!"

"I can't," you explain. "I just don't feel like it. Chris might want to talk or something. You know, he's going through a tough time right now."

Mira sighs. "I heard he still hasn't broken up with Amy."

"Well, he's working on it. He doesn't want to break her heart or anything," you say, defending him. "I think that means that he's a really good guy."

"I hope you can trust him, that's all I'm saying."
Mira looks so serious.

"I can trust him," you tell her. "He's practically
my boyfriend!"

Later that night, you watch a movie that you
rented and make some popcorn. You hope that
Mira and Kelly are having fun at the dance. And you
hope that Chris isn't too sad tonight. You decide to
cheer him up with a quick call on his cell, but when
he doesn't pick up, you just leave a sweet message.
"Let me know if you want me to come over tonight,"
you say to his voice mail. "I can if you want to talk,
or whatever."

About two minutes later, your cell phone rings,
and you just know it's going to be him! But when
you pick up, it's Mira. "Hey," you say. You can hear
loud music and talking in the background.

"Hey, it's me," she says. "Can you hear me?"

"Barely," you laugh. "You guys having fun?"

"Not really," Mira says. "I have to tell you something. Chris is here."

"He is?" You sit up on the couch, surprised. He
told you he wasn't going! But maybe he thought
you were going to be there or something.

"And he's not alone. He's here with Amy. They

are totally together. He's a liar, and a total jerk!" Mira yells over the background noise of the dance.

"What?" you can't believe this, she must be joking. "He's there with her?"

"They were just crowned King and Queen of the dance! I'm telling you, he's a dog," she says. "Please don't believe anything else he tells you."

You hang up the phone in shock. How could he do this to you? You wish you could go back and redo your whole relationship with him. How could you have fallen for someone who would treat you this badly?

END

If you want to give up on Chris once and for all,
    go back to 104.

$\mathcal{Y}$ou push Kristen's hand away from your dress, then put your hands on her shoulders and shove her backward. "Don't touch me!" you yell at her.

"You keep your hands off of me!" she screeches back at you, and grabs a handful of your hair.

"Stop it!" Mira yells, trying to separate the two of you.

"Catfight!" You hear a guy yell, and a crowd starts forming.

Kristen pulls your hair—hard!—so you put your hand in her face and push her back. She stumbles and falls, taking you with her! You try your best to get away, but she's still got your hair in her fist and she tugs you down. You feel your elbow go into her ribs as you fall on her, and she lets out a scream, but finally lets go of your hair. As you scramble to get up, you hear a loud tearing sound and feel yourself fall forward.

"My dress!" you scream as you look down and realize that she's torn off the whole lower half of your perfect dress—and your pink and white polka-dot panties are on display for the entire school! You cover your face with your hands and make a dash for the girls' bathroom. But as you race off the dance floor, you hear all the boys hooting and clapping.

"Nice undies!" someone shouts.

How on Earth are you ever going to show your face at school again?

END

If you want to rethink that fight with Kristen, go back to 134.

You push Kristen's hand away from your dress. "What are you trying to do?" you ask her. "I'm not getting into a fight with you over this." And you turn and walk away from her.

"I'm not done talking to you!" Kristen yells, and starts following you onto the dance floor.

"Look, leave me alone," you tell her, "or I'll get one of the teachers to make sure you leave me alone. Got it?"

"You're such a baby," Kristen taunts you. "Go run and tattle, tell the teacher!" She stands with her hands on her hips, daring you to say something back. But you don't. You just turn and move to another part of the dance floor with your friends.

"I think she's seriously insane!" Mira says.

"What's the big deal?" Kelly says. "So you are both wearing the same dress. It's not the end of the world."

"It is for her," Mira laughs. "Because you look so much better in it!"

You have to laugh—you're so lucky to have two best friends like Mira and Kelly. What would you do without them?

"Hi," you hear someone say, and look over to see Chris, the hottie football player, standing right next to you. He's wearing a dark suit jacket that looks great against his golden skin and shaggy blond hair.

"Hey." You nod at him, looking around for his girlfriend—you almost got in one fight tonight; you don't need another girl mad at you!

"I like your dress. You look … great, really great." Chris smiles at you. You love the way his eyes light up when he's talking to you.

"Thanks," you say warily. You notice that Mira and Kelly have made themselves scarce and are now watching you—while pretending that they aren't watching you—from across the room.

"Would you like to dance? I mean, you *are* dancing, but would you like to dance with me?" Chris asks.

"I would," you say, "but you have a girlfriend and I don't think she'd like it too much." You smile.

"I don't have a girlfriend anymore," Chris says,

pointing across the dance floor to where his ex is dancing with another guy from the football team. "We broke up last week. Actually, it was over a while ago, but I guess neither one of us wanted to deal with it."

"I'm sorry," you say. He doesn't look too upset about it.

"It's okay," Chris says. "It's sort of funny, when we broke up, we both admitted that we had crushes on other people," Chris says, looking down into your eyes for a second. "The guy she's with now, he's actually a friend of mine, but … it's weird, 'cause I'm okay with it."

"Really?" you ask him. You find it hard to believe that he could get over her so fast—they dated for more than a year!

"Yeah, really. But that's probably because I like someone else, too," he says, giving you a smile. "I don't really know her very well, but I want to.…" He trails off, looking into your eyes. You can't believe it—he's talking about *you*! The song stops, and suddenly a slow song begins as the lights in the gym dim down. A lot of people leave the dance floor, so only couples surround you and Chris now.

"So, how about that dance?" he asks again.

"Okay," you say, blushing as you take his hand.

For a night that almost started with a huge fight, things have certainly turned out pretty well for you!

END

"I'd love to go!" you say, turning to look at Eddie's face. Is he into it or not? You're not scared to party with the older kids. It might be fun!

"Sounds cool," Eddie says, grinning. "Let us know when you're leaving and we can all ride over together in the limo."

"Awesome, let's party!" Owen yells, and spins Mira on the dance floor.

You dance to a few more songs, and then Owen comes over to you and Eddie with some news. "My friend's brother just called. He says the party is raging—let's go now, before all the beer is gone!"

"Okay," you say, even though you sort of wanted to stay at the dance longer—you're having a great time just hanging out with Eddie. Who cares what everyone else is doing?

"I'll go grab Mira," Owen says, and dashes off.

Once he's out of earshot, Eddie takes your hand. "Do you really want to go to this party?"

"I thought I did...," you start to say.

"If you're just going because you think I want to

go, you're wrong," he says softly. "I don't need to be at some raging party to have fun."

"But all of our friends are going," you say, looking up at him. You don't want him to miss out just because of you.

Eddie shrugs. "Friends, whatever. I'd rather be with my girlfriend."

It takes you a second to realize that he's talking about *you!* "Girlfriend?" You hear yourself repeat the word.

"Yeah, girlfriend." Eddie smiles at you. "Come on, let's keep dancing. Those guys can find another ride." He takes your hand and leads you back onto the dance floor. As a slow song starts playing, he holds you close. And when you put your cheek against his chest, you can feel his heart beating. Eddie isn't just your best guy friend anymore—he's your boyfriend (and you couldn't be happier!).

END

$\mathcal{B}$efore you can say no, Eddie quickly says, "Sounds great! In fact, when you guys are ready to roll, come grab us, and we'll all ride over to the party in the limo!"

"Awesome!" Owen yells. "Prepare to party!" He high-fives Eddie, then grabs Mira and swings her onto the dance floor.

"Dance?" Eddie asks, grabbing your arm, but you just shake your head. "What's up? Is something wrong?"

You love the way Eddie can always tell what you're thinking—must be because you were friends for so long. "I'm not so sure about the party... I mean, you can go, and I don't want to ruin your night or anything, if you're into that kind of thing, or whatever—"

"Are you kidding?" Eddie asks. He puts his hand under your chin and tilts your face up so that he can look into your eyes. "All I want to do tonight is hang out with you. Wherever you are. I don't care if we spend the rest of the night at the taco stand; I just want to be with you and have fun!"

"Really?" you ask. "So you don't mind skipping the party?"

"Really. We'll drop those guys off and go grab something to eat instead."

"Tacos?" you ask, jokingly.

"Si, señorita," he says, and leans in to kiss you softly on the lips. Amazing how Eddie has gone from your best guy friend to boyfriend so quickly—and you couldn't be happier!

END

The next day after school, you and Kelly both go over to Tyler's house to hear his band play.

"Do you really think they'll be any good?" Kelly asks you as you get off the bus.

"I hope so." You grin at her.

"You are too far gone!" Kelly laughs.

The guys set up in the garage and start jamming. You find yourself lost in the music again—you can't take your eyes off of Tyler—he's that amazing. "They're perfect!" she yells to you over the music.

And when you tell Tyler after the band wraps up, he's ecstatic. "You're kidding! Our first real gig? And we're being paid?" He grabs you up in a giant bear hug and dances you around the garage.

But the next day after school, he doesn't have any time to hang out. "I've got practice with the guys for the dance," he explains, dashing for his friend's car. "See ya!" As the weekend of the big dance grows closer, you realize that even though you have a huge crush on Tyler—and you got him the gig—he's not even technically your date to the dance. In fact, he can't take a date, because he's in the band! Oops, what have you done?

☙❧

The night of the dance, you go over to Kelly's house to get ready. Mira and Kel are beyond excited about all the cute boys who will be there. "Do you think I'll see Owen? Will he be there with someone?" Mira asks, leaning in to the mirror to put on some eyeliner. Kelly is too busy blow-drying her hair to answer. "Should I ask him to dance?" Mira asks, turning to you. "What do you think?" You just shrug, realizing that you'll have no one to dance with—the guy you're into will be onstage playing with the band!

When you get to the dance, the band is already setting up. Tyler looks adorable in jeans, a cool T-shirt, and a funky jacket, but you can tell from the look on his face that he's nervous. "You guys are going to be great," you go over and tell him.

"You think so?" he asks, meeting your eyes for a second.

"I know so," you tell him with a smile. Even if you can't be his date, you're proud of him.

When they start playing, everyone tunes in and a bunch of people hit the dance floor right away. Kelly and Mira pull you in to dance, too. You're so into the music that you almost don't hear the girl next to you saying, "Who's that lead singer? Yum!" Is she talking about *your* Tyler?

You look up to the stage and meet his eyes for a second, then he looks back down at his guitar strings with a smile. Kelly's right—you've totally fallen for him!

The song ends and you find yourself out of breath from dancing. Then you see Tyler lean in to the microphone. "Thanks, everyone, we're psyched to be here playing at the dance and hope you're happy to have us," he says. The crowd lets out a big cheer and Kelly turns to you and nods. "They are *so* perfect!" she says.

You turn your attention back to Tyler just in time to hear him say, "This next song goes out to my girl." He points at you, and you feel everyone turn to look. "I wrote this for you," he says. His eyes lock onto yours.

You can't believe it. He wrote a song for you? The rest of the band stands by quietly while he starts to play the guitar, singing beautiful lyrics about a girl who believed in him when no one else did—that's you! When the song ends, everyone claps loudly, and you feel so lightheaded—is this love? The dance that you weren't even looking forward to is turning out to be the best night of your life!

END

You really don't want to tell Tyler that Kelly didn't love the idea of his band playing at the dance. After you get off the phone with her, you get an e-mail from Tyler saying that he had fun hanging out with you and that he's excited to hear what Kelly thinks of the idea. You can't even write him back because you're too afraid to hurt his feelings.

When you see Tyler at school the next day, he makes his way over to you in the hall and corners you at your locker. "So, what's up? Did you talk to Kelly?" he asks, searching your eyes. You look up and meet his gaze. "I'm really sorry, but Kelly wasn't that into the idea," you tell him.

"Oh," he says, looking bummed. "Well, there will be other gigs. It's no big deal," he finally says.

"Really?" you ask. "You're not mad?" You're feeling guilty that you didn't fight for him more.

He looks into your face. "I can't believe you even thought I was talented enough to ask Kelly at all. Nobody has ever done anything like that for me. Why would I be mad?" he asks you. "And look at it this way, since I won't be playing at the dance, that means I can take you to the dance as my date, right?"

You meet his dark green eyes and smile. "I guess that's a good way to look at it," you admit.

Who would have thought the oddball guy from the committee meeting would end up being your date to the dance!

END

You could never ask Mr. Marshall to carry you, so instead you just hobble out to the parking lot as best you can. When you get out there, you see all the bake sale tables and other fund-raisers set up—including the dunking booth, filled with water and just waiting for you! *Eek*!

As you carefully climb the stairs to the bench where you're supposed to sit, Mr. Marshall holds your arm. "Good luck, mermaid," he says to you. "And thanks again for doing this—really shows your school spirit!"

You manage a tiny smile as you take your seat and look out over the crowd of students. Oh no! The first one in line to take a chance at dunking you is Sean, the hot football player! Why did it have to be him!?

"Hey, mermaid, better hold your breath!" you hear someone yell, and someone else lets out a low whistle. Maybe this wasn't such a good idea. Before you even have time to think about it, Sean takes a shot—and hits the target! *SPLASH*—you're under the cold water in a second. As you struggle to stand up in your very wet mermaid costume, you realize that you forgot to wear waterproof mascara today. Oops.

You climb back up onto the bench and look to see who is next in line. But Sean is still standing there! "I bought three turns," he yells up to you. "I wanted to make sure you went swimming today!" he laughs, throwing his next ball. He hits the target again, and with a loud *SPLASH,* you're back in the water. This time, it takes you a second to get your footing in the booth and you slip—almost toppling over as you go under the water again.

In a flash, Sean races up the stairs of the booth to grab your arm. "You okay?" he says. "Here, let me help," he says, lifting you onto the bench.

"Thanks," you say, then, meeting his eyes angrily, you add, "I *guess.*"

"Are you really mad?" he asks, looking worried. "It's a fund-raiser, right? I'm just doing my part to help out the school. How was I supposed to know you were going to show up looking adorable in that costume?"

You let out a laugh. "Adorable? I look like a drowned rat!" you say, pushing your wet hair back from your makeup-streaked face.

"Then you're the cutest rat I've ever seen," Sean

says quietly. "Here," he hands you the last ball he's holding. "I'll trade places with you, and you can try to dunk me, okay?"

You look down at the baseball—the idea *is* tempting.

"Come on! We're waiting!" someone from the line yells.

"Yeah, it's my turn to dunk the mermaid!" another guy shouts out.

"That's okay," you tell Sean. "I think the crowd wants to dunk the mystery mermaid, not the star football player. Besides, I don't think the costume would fit you," you laugh.

"You're probably right." Sean grins. "But I have to make it up to you somehow. Maybe you'll let me take you to the dance next weekend—you can even wear the mermaid look if you want."

"I'll think about it," you say, meeting his eyes for a moment. But you already know what your answer will be. Looks like mermaids really *are* magical!

172

END

That night, you call Kelly. "Listen, I don't think the committee I'm on is going to work out, but I still want to help with the dance. Can you put me on another committee or something?"

"Sure," Kelly says. "Would you rather be on the decorating committee?"

"Sounds perfect," you say.

"I'll work it out. Tomorrow, why don't you plan to meet Sean after school to start things with Mr. Marshall, okay?" Kelly asks.

"I'll be there. Thanks, Kel," you tell her.

173

Go to 174.

The next day after school, you meet up with Sean. "Let's go and see if Mr. Marshall is still here; maybe he's in the art room," Sean says. As you walk to Mr. Marshall's class, Sean asks your name and what grade you're in.

"I don't think I've seen you around," he says, shooting you a look. "I guess we don't have any classes together."

"No, but I've seen you on the football team," you point out. "You're really good."

"Oh yeah?" he says, looking a little sheepish. "Thanks."

When you get to the art room, Mr. Marshall is still there. "Hey, guys," he says, obviously happy to see you.

"We were at the dance planning meeting yesterday," Sean says, "and I guess we're supposed to talk to you about decorating."

"Great," Mr. Marshall says quickly. You notice that when he smiles, he has the most adorable dimples, and you start wondering how old he is...and if he's married. "I think we need to talk about fund-raising first—we'll need the funds to decorate the gym, since the school doesn't have a budget for that."

"Right," Sean says. "I can help decorate the gym, but I'm really busy with the football team right now, so I don't think I can help much with fund-raising. Maybe some of the other kids on the committee can?"

Mr. Marshall turns to you with a warm smile. "What do you say? Do you want to help me with the fund-raising, or can you only decorate the gym, too?"

You can just imagine how fun it would be to help Mr. Marshall with the fund-raising—or with anything, for that matter! You just want to hang out with him. But he *is* a teacher, hardly a candidate for a date to the dance! So you decide to...

Do fund-raising with Mr. Marshall. Go to 38.
Just decorate with Sean. Go to 40.

Check out:

Date Him or Dump Him?
The Campfire Crush

Last summer, you were just another camper at Camp Butterfield. But this year, everything's different because you're finally a junior counselor! There is so much to look forward to, like having your pick of cabins and bonding with your young campers, not to mention a LOT of cute guys. But besides the prospect of pairing up with your crush for lifeguard training, or flirting with another counselor on a whitewater rafting trip, there are snakes to get rid of, poison ivy to avoid, and plenty of trails to follow—all leading to love . . . you hope!

And read on for
a sneak peek at:

Date Him or Dump Him?
Ski Trip Trouble

The big school field trip to Mount Frost is finally here! You and your best friend, Heather, can't wait to hit the slopes, hang out in the lodge, and check out all the cute guys from the neighboring school.... But in between braving the black diamond run with an old crush and sipping a steamy cup of cocoa with a sweet younger guy, you've got

snowball fights to win, a whole town to explore, and even—gulp!—a karaoke night to attend. Will you ski your way to a sweetheart or be left out in the cold? It's all up to you!

Coming soon!

1

It's another cold, gray day when you get to school on Thursday morning. Winter break is just two weeks away, but before you can relax and take some time off from school, there are all those end-of-the-semester tests, papers, and projects due. Thank goodness it's the school ski trip this weekend, otherwise you'd be going out of your mind with stress! Before you even go to your first class, you head over to the main bulletin board to check out the sign-up sheet for the ski trip one more time.

"I can't believe it's finally here!" your friend Heather says as she comes up behind you. "Tomorrow—no school, we just hit the mountain. I cannot wait!"

"Look at this," you say, pointing to one name on the list.

"Dan's going? Wasn't he, like, in love with you last year?" Heather jokes, and you have to laugh.

"I guess so." You grin. "But now I hear he likes somebody else."

Heather blushes. "I don't know about that!"

"Oh please, he follows you around everywhere, just like he used to do with me," you say, but Heather just looks down at her shoes shyly. "And I'm getting the feeling that you might like him back...."

"Maybe just a little," she admits, pinching her thumb and forefinger together.

"I guess a romantic ski trip to the snowy slopes will help you figure it out!" you joke, hooking your arm through hers. "We better get to class," you say, just as the warning bell rings.

"Did you hear that Marshall High is also going to Mount Frost this weekend?" Heather asks you with a sly grin.

"You know I did," you say back, "because you're the one who told me!"

"I just can't help wondering if a certain former crush is going to be there," Heather goes on.

"Look, I haven't seen Mitch since he moved away over the summer," you explain. "It's been months." You stop outside the door to your classroom. "And just because his new school is going on this trip, it doesn't mean *he's* going to be there."

"Uh-huh," Heather says, cocking her head to one side. "So the thought hasn't even crossed your mind? You and Mitch, sipping hot chocolate, talking about those long days at the pool last summer, that time when you almost kissed..."

You move to swat her with your backpack, but she jumps back just in time. "Knock it off!" You laugh. "Seriously, what if he's not even there?"

"I have a feeling he will be," Heather teases as the final bell rings. "Eek! I'm late!"

"Call me tonight—let's talk about what we're going to pack, okay?" you yell after her as she races down the hall.

"Okay! Later," she yells back.

❧

Very early the next morning—when it's still practically dark out—you meet up with Heather and all the other students going on the ski trip.

"I feel like a snowman in this thing," Heather says, patting the front of her big, puffy white jacket.

"I know what you mean," you say, zipping up

your own coat. Mrs. Bulow, the teacher who organized the trip, comes over to the group crowded around the bus.

"Everyone, listen up!" she says, clapping her gloved hands together. "I'm going to be the head chaperone on this trip. If you have any problems or issues, come to me."

"I have an issue," Heather whispers to you. "I'm freezing to death! When do we get on the bus?"

You can feel your feet getting numb—it *is* a really cold morning.

"We have two other teachers coming along on the trip, and we have four seniors from the school who have volunteered to be junior chaperones." Mrs. Bulow points to the guys standing next to her. "This is James," she says, introducing a tall guy with dark hair. "And this is Glenn," she goes on, "and Max," she says, pointing to a blond guy in a puffy down vest standing next to her. "And of course, Cathy." She motions to the petite girl on her other side. "All of these students are seniors and have been on the school ski trip in the past. And they are all excellent skiers."

"Excellent indeed...," you hear Heather murmur next to you.

"Shhhhh," you whisper back, but she's right—the guys are all amazingly hot.

"What?" Heather says. "Like you wouldn't die for that guy to ride the chairlift with you?" She nods at the dark-haired senior.

You take another glance at him—just when he happens to look your way! You quickly look down.

"Busted!" Heather says under her breath. You feel your cheeks turning even redder as Mrs. Bulow goes on.

"Respect the junior chaperones. They are not just fellow students; they are here to look out for you. Treat them exactly the same way you would treat us teachers," she says, motioning to the two other teachers standing near her.

Heather starts doing a little dance from one foot to the other, trying to keep warm, just as Mrs. Bulow happens to look over. "Does anyone need to use the bathroom before we go?" she asks, and a few of the boys in the group start laughing. "It is a two-hour trip," she says, looking pointedly at you and Heather. Heather stops hopping. "Oh man, could she embarrass us more?"

"I know it's cold out here—let's line up and climb on the bus!" Mrs. Bulow finally says, and everyone races for the door. When you and Heather finally make your way up the stairs into the bus, almost every seat is taken. "Here?" Heather says, pointing to a seat right behind the driver. It's not exactly the best seat, but you don't really have any other choice—the bus is totally packed.

When everyone is sitting, Mrs. Bulow comes onboard. "We have a tiny problem," she starts. "I need to ride on the bus, too, but as you can see, it's full. So I need someone to give me their seat and ride up to the mountain in the van with the junior chaperones."

"Let's do it," Heather whispers to you, nudging your arm.

"We'll volunteer," you say quickly. "Heather and I don't mind."

"Yeah, no problem," Heather agrees, standing up and grabbing her backpack.

"Sorry, girls, I only need *one* of you to give up your seat," Mrs. Bulow points out. "And there's only room for one person in the van, too. But if you don't mind going alone"—she looks directly at you—"this seat *would* be perfect for me, right up front where I can keep an eye on everyone."

You look over at Heather. "It's up to you," she

says, though you're sure she'd rather not have to sit by Mrs. Bulow for the two-hour bus ride. You can't help thinking about that junior chaperone, James, and how cool it would be to get to know him better. You look back at Heather. It *is* just a ride up the mountain, after all, and you'll get to hang out with Heather for the rest of the weekend....

"Let's get a move on here!" the bus driver says, turning around to look at you. "In or out, missy?" He pulls the handle to open the bus door, and a rush of cold air comes in, hitting your face. You take a deep breath and decide to...

Stay on the bus with Heather. Go to 2.

Join the junior chaperones in the van. Go to 3.

2

"I think I'd rather stay on the bus with my friend," you tell Mrs. Bulow.

"I'll go," a guy sitting across from you quickly volunteers.

"Perfect!" Mrs. Bulow says.

"See you up there, suckers!" the guy yells as he goes out the door of the bus.

"What a loser," Heather whispers to you.

"He's probably right, though—the van will make it up there a lot faster than this old bus," you say.

"Are you wishing you'd gone in the van?" Heather asks, looking hurt.

"No, I'm just saying...," you start, but then notice someone leaning over you—it's Dan.

"Hey," he says, pushing his shaggy blond hair back from his eyes. "I was just wondering if maybe I could sit with Heather," he asks, looking at you.

"Um..." You're about to say no, but then notice that Heather is giving you a hopeful look. Maybe you should have gone in the van after all! "Sure, I can move," you mumble.

"Great!" Heather says.

"I was sitting right back there." Dan points back to the only empty seat, and you make your way down the aisle as he sits next to Heather. When you get to the back of the bus, you realize that Dan had been sitting with this cute guy—all you know about him is that he skipped a grade and he's supposed to be super smart.

"Is it okay if I sit here?" you ask him. "Dan wanted to move up front."

Go to 5.

$$3$$

"Okay, I'll ride in the van," you tell Mrs. Bulow. You hear Heather let out a sigh, so you turn to her. "I'll see you up there," you explain. "Please don't be mad."

"I'm not." Heather smiles. "Just wish I was coming, too. Say hi to James for me, 'kay?" she winks.

"No problem," you say as you go down the stairs and leave the bus. The driver follows you and opens the luggage compartment. You see your bag right on top and grab it. "Thanks," you tell the driver with a wave as he climbs back onto the bus.

You walk over to the van and hear music blasting out of the open doors. "Hi! Mrs. Bulow asked me to ride up with you guys," you tell the girl junior chaperone.

"Cool," she says, grabbing your bag and tossing it into the back of the van. "I'm Cathy. You can sit with me while this maniac drives." She gives James a little punch in the arm.

"Maniac on the slopes," James corrects her. "Behind the wheel, never." He grins over at you. "Hey, I'm James," he says, putting out his hand,

and you tell him your name.

"Let's go, people!" says Mr. Abbott, one of the teachers chaperoning the trip, motioning everyone into the van. You sit next to Cathy in the first row of backseats, while the two other seniors sit behind you. When James goes to sit in the driver's seat, Mr. Abbot says, "Not so fast," and grabs the keys from him. "I'll be doing the driving."

James grumbles but sits in the passenger seat and instantly starts messing with the CD player. "Okay, passengers, what do we want to hear? Some death rock, acid beats?"

You let out a laugh because you assume he's joking—he doesn't really listen to that type of music, does he? In a second, you realize you're wrong as James slips in a disc of the worst music you've ever heard.

"These guys and their heavy metal," Cathy grumbles to you over the loud music. She puts on her own headphones and starts listening to her MP3 player, looking out the window. By the time Mr. Abbott pulls the van out onto the freeway, you already have a headache.

"This album is so rad—this is the best ski music ever!" you hear Glenn, the other junior chaperone, say from behind you.

"Get ready to party!" James says loudly, and Mr. Abbott shoots him a look.

"Can you please turn that noise down?" Mr. Abbott asks. "I'm trying to drive, here."

"Noise?" James says. "This is one of the greatest heavy metal albums of all time!" He turns around in his seat and looks at you. "You dig it, right? I mean, how awesome are these guitar licks?" James plays air guitar along with the song for a second, and you almost burst out laughing. Even if his taste in music is terrible, he's still adorable.

"It's not exactly my type of music," you tell him, smiling.

"When we get up to the mountain, we'll teach you how to really party," James says, knowingly. "Right, dude?" he says to Glenn, and gives him a thumbs up.

"Righteous!" Glenn yells over the music.

Are these guys for real?

"Oh no," you hear Mr. Abbott say suddenly, as the van starts making a funny thumping sound—*chug-chug-chug*—and then it stops altogether! "Sorry, guys, I thought this van might give us trouble," Mr. Abbott says as he pulls over to the side of the highway. The van comes to a stop, and Mr.

Abbott turns around. "I'll go have a look at the engine, but I think we may need to call a tow truck." His face looks glum as he climbs out of the van. He lifts the hood, and black smoke comes billowing out of the engine!

"That's not good," James jokes.

Mr. Abbott pokes his head back into the van for a second. "The bus is coming up the hill right behind us, so if any of you want to flag down the driver and get on, feel free. This looks like it's going to take a while," he explains.

You want to get up to the mountain so that you can ski this afternoon with your friends, but you were also looking forward to this road trip with James the cutie. You look over to him for a second. "I'm staying, man. The bus is for losers!" he says.

"Here comes the bus. Anyone want me to flag it down?" Mr. Abbott says again, and you decide to...

Stay and wait for the repairs on the van. Go to 6.

Flag down the bus and squeeze on. Go to . . . your local bookstore for *Ski Trip Trouble*!

4

"Great," the guy says. You tap Zac on the shoulder, and when he slips off his headphones, you quickly explain what's up.

"So I'll see you later," you say as you move over to sit by Molly.

"Definitely." Zac grins back. Looks like you've made at least one new friend on this trip already!

Once you get settled into your new seat, you turn to Molly. "You're new at school, right?" After the words are out of your mouth, you feel silly. Obviously she's new!

"Yeah," she says, nodding. "We used to live a couple of towns over, so it's not that different."

"But it must have been hard to leave all your friends," you continue.

"That wasn't easy, but I still see them sometimes. Actually, some of my old friends from middle school go to Marshall now. One of my best friends, Sierra, is going on this trip—I'm psyched to meet her up there."

"How cool," you say, but just the mention of the

other high school instantly makes you think of Mitch. "I have a friend from last year who goes to Marshall. So maybe he'll be there, too," you tell her.

She raises her eyebrows. "Friend? Or boyfriend?" she says with a grin.

"Well…" You feel your cheeks flush as you struggle to answer.

"You don't have to explain," Molly says, pulling her long blond hair into a high ponytail. "I know all about those kinds of friends!"

You realize that Molly is actually really easy to talk to—she's funny and super nice, too. "When we get up there, do you want to room together?" she asks. "I don't really have any friends on this trip, so I was just going to stay with whoever was left."

You had been planning to stay with Heather and her friend Carrie, but it might be fun to room with a new friend—especially one who has Marshall connections! And Heather is so wrapped up with her crush on Dan, she probably wouldn't even notice…but then again, she is your best friend….

You'd rather stay with Heather. Go to … your local library for *Ski Trip Touble*!

You want to room with the new girl, Molly. Go to … an online book retailer for *Ski Trip Trouble*!

"Sure," he says, "I don't think we've ever met, but I'm Zac." You tell him your name and he quickly responds, "Oh, I know who you are—I thought that project you did in English last week was really amazing."

"Thanks." You smile. You had thought it was pretty cool, but none of your friends even mentioned it to you. "So, you skipped a grade or something, right?" you ask him.

"Yeah, the teachers thought it might be a good idea, so I was bumped up," he says, looking out the window. It seems like he doesn't really want to talk about it, but you're so curious.

"How is it going? Is it really hard to keep up?" you ask.

"I'm only a year younger than everybody else, so it's not that big a deal," he explains. "But *some* people want to make it a big deal, you know?"

You nod and glance over at the popular kids, all sitting together in a group. "Yeah, I know what you mean," you tell him.

"Anyway," he says, looking at your MP3 player, "what are you listening to?"

You two start talking about—and listening to—music, and before you know it, a half hour has gone by. You're listening to his MP3 player, and he's checking out yours, when the guy sitting across the aisle from you leans over and taps your shoulder.

"Hey, would you mind switching seats with me?" he asks. "Zac is my tutor at school and I need to ask him some homework questions."

You glance over to Zac, but he's got headphones on and hasn't noticed anything. You look back at the guy and see that he's sitting with Molly, the new girl at school. You've noticed her in your art class, and she seems really cool. This could be your chance to meet her. But you also really like sitting with Zac and getting to know him.

You tell the guy…

ℓ

"Sure, I'll switch seats with you." Go to 4.

"Sorry, Zac's busy right now. You'll have to ask him later."

Go to . . . your school library for *Ski Trip Trouble*!

6

"That's okay, Mr. Abbott," you say. "I'll just wait with everyone else." As the bus roars by, a few kids make faces through the windows. So what if they'll get up the mountain before you? At least you get to hang with a group of cool seniors!

Before too long, the repair crew shows up with a tow truck. "Sorry, mister," the driver says to Mr. Abbott. "This van isn't going anywhere. We can have a rental vehicle sent out, but we'll have to tow this one back to the garage."

"Okay," Mr. Abbott says. "I guess we don't really have much choice. Everyone please get your bags out of the back."

Cathy opens the back of the van and starts piling up the bags on the side of the road, but as she puts one big duffel bag down, you hear a loud *clink* and the sound of glass breaking. "Oops," Cathy says, cringing, as a dark syrupy liquid starts leaking through the bag. "What's that?"

In a few seconds, there's a puddle of something

under the bag, and it smells sweet—and strange, like…

"Is that what I think it is?" Mr. Abbott says, taking a sniff. He unzips the bag to reveal a four-pack of wine coolers, two of the bottles broken. "Whose bag is this?" he asks, and no one says anything. "Yours?" he turns to Glenn.

Glenn just looks down.

"Glenn, show me which bag is yours," Mr. Abbott says, and he sounds angry.

"Hmm," Glenn says, looking over the bags. "I really can't remember right now."

Mr. Abbott glares at him. "Cathy, which one is yours?" he asks.

"Gosh, Mr. Abbott," she says, "I can't tell; they all look alike." She gives James a nudge. You know what they're doing—no one is going to take the blame.

Mr. Abbott points to you. "Which bag is yours? And stop playing games!"

You look down at the bags, then up at James, who gives you a sly smile. If you play along, then maybe no one will get in trouble. But you shouldn't get in trouble, anyway—you didn't do anything wrong! Do you want to cover for James and his friends, or tell the truth and point out your bag?

You lie and say you can't remember which bag is yours. Go to . . . a book club for *Ski Trip Trouble*!

You show Mr. Abbott your bag. Go to . . . *Ski Trip Trouble*, coming to bookstores, libraries, online retailers, book clubs, and all other places books are available—SOON!

ᖯCYLIN ᖯBUSBYᖰ

first chose a life as a book and magazine editor, before
going back a page and becoming a full-time writer instead.
She lives with two boys of her own choosing—Damon, her
husband, and August, her son, in Los Angeles.

The life of an Inside Girl is anything but ordinary.

Find out what it's like in this fun new series by J. Minter, the creator of *The Insiders*.

Flan Flood has always had her pick of the coolest parties and the cutest designer clothes. Her family is legendary in New York City, but she's sick of her friends hanging around just to get closer to her hot older brother, Patch. So when Flan starts at a new high school, she decides to reinvent herself as a totally normal girl. The only problem is, Flan's life isn't exactly normal. What will happen when her two worlds collide?

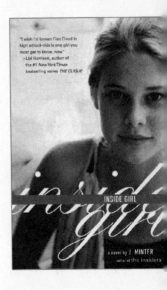

"I wish I'd known Flan Flood in high school—and not just because she has a hot older brother with hot older friends (although that totally helps). Don't let the name fool you—this is one girl you must get to know, now."

—Lisi Harrison, author of *The Clique*

Learn more about Flan and the Inside Girls at www.insidegirlbooks.com